THE STORY OF MARCO

By Eleanor H. Porter

Cover Design by Elle Staples

Cover Illustration by Dan Burr

First published in 1911

© 2018 Jenny Phillips

This version has updated grammar and spelling and has has lessened slang in some places.

This version is unabridged, but the ending chapters have been reordered and modified.

TABLE OF CONTENTS

CHAPTER 1 1
CHAPTER 2 4
CHAPTER 3 9
CHAPTER 4 13
CHAPTER 5 16
CHAPTER 6 20
CHAPTER 7 28
CHAPTER 8 34
CHAPTER 9 38
CHAPTER 10 42
CHAPTER 11 45
CHAPTER 12 50
CHAPTER 13 54
CHAPTER 14 57
CHAPTER 15 61
CHAPTER 16 65
CHAPTER 17 69
CHAPTER 18 75
CHAPTER 19 79
CHAPTER 20 85
CHAPTER 21 90
CHAPTER 22 93
CHAPTER 23 99
CHAPTER 24 104
CHAPTER 25 109
CHAPTER 26 115
CHAPTER 27 119
CHAPTER 28 123
CHAPTER 29 126
CHAPTER 30 132
CHAPTER 31 135
CHAPTER 32 142
CHAPTER 33 154
CHAPTER 34 160
CHAPTER 35 164
CHAPTER 36 167

CHAPTER 1

Marco Ferdinando Bonelli—otherwise, "Bonesy"—peered cautiously through the underbrush at the mouth of the cave and then stepped out into the sunlight.

Below him the hill fell away in a sheer descent of three hundred feet to a little clearing where a wide area of trampled grass around a small gray tent told of a much larger encampment earlier in the day. With a half-stifled cry, the boy tightened his grasp on the battered violin case in his hand and plunged through the underbrush to where a stony path led by a devious way to the foot of the hill. Some minutes later he bounded into the clearing and began softly to approach the tent. He had almost reached it when, as if the idea had suddenly come to him, he stopped and opened his violin case. A moment later a weird, curious melody broke the silence of the clearing.

Almost instantly at the door of the tent appeared a woman, blue-eyed, fair-haired, and with two vivid red spots on otherwise colorless cheeks.

"Marco? Why, Marco! What does this mean?" she cried.

The boy did not reply, but the music lost its minor wail and burst suddenly into joyful strains of triumphant runs and double-stopping—which, after all, was more eloquent than any words could have been.

"But, Marco, my son," cried the woman again, "why did you come back?"

This time the music stopped. The boy smiled exultingly and lowered his violin.

"I didn't go," he retorted.

"Didn't go! Where were you?"

"Up there." He jerked his thumb toward the hidden cave.

"But, Marco, they hunted everywhere for you. They thought you'd gone ahead. I was frightened."

The boy's face changed. All the brightness fled from it and left it suddenly old and troubled. He frowned angrily. "I didn't mean to scare you," he protested, "but I heard them talk about me goin' and leavin' you. As if I'd do that!"

The woman sighed and sank to a low stool near the tent door. She began to cough painfully, and it was some minutes before she found her breath to speak again. Meanwhile, the boy watched her, his young eyes deep and troubled.

"But, dearie, I'm going—right along—soon, too," she panted.

"All right. I'll go then, but I won't leave you now—like them!" His lips snapped together over the last word, and his stormy eyes sought the grassy lane that led to the highway, down which that morning had disappeared the hurrying, gesticulating band of gypsies.

"But they had to go, Marco," defended the woman, feebly. "The townspeople would not let them stay."

There was a long silence. The boy was sitting now at the woman's feet, his fingers idly caressing the satiny smoothness of his violin.

"Mumsey," he asked abruptly, after a time, "be you a gypsy?"

"No, but I married one."

"Where is he—Dad?"

A sudden flame leaped to the woman's eyes. "I don't know," she answered.

The boy changed his position. Something in his mother's face did not encourage further questioning, and after a moment he picked up his violin and began to play softly.

Over in the west the sun dropped behind the hills, and only the treetops showed a golden glow. The grass became a deeper, more vivid green, and the shadows grew darker under the trees; even into the boy's playing crept a touch of the twilight hush.

Gradually the angry light faded from the woman's eyes. It was quite gone when she finally lifted her head and dragged herself to her feet.

"Come, come, Marco, it's supper time. They left me food—plenty of it—to last a week, and long before that I'll be better and well enough to follow them. Then we'll go, won't we? Why, Marco, I'm better already!" she finished, with the optimism that is so often a running mate to the disease that paints the treacherous roses on its victim's cheeks.

The boy stopped playing. His eyes were wistful. For a moment he did not speak. Then he sighed, "Mumsey, wouldn't it be just perfect in this great green stillness if only Flossie were here?"

The woman caught her breath sharply. "They wouldn't leave her, anyhow, and they didn't think they'd left you," she almost sobbed. "They said I couldn't take care of kids—as if my children could trouble me! Besides, I'm better, Marco. Why, I'm lots better! I was almost well enough to go with them today."

"Of course you're better," declared Marco stoutly, as he followed his mother into the tent.

In the long twilight they sat again outside the tent and watched the stars come out one by one, and the great round moon raised its golden disk above the treetops. They talked, too—at least Marco talked, and he drew a glowing picture of all the good things that were to come to his "little mumsey" when he should be a man. Then he took up his violin and began to play, and into the runs and trills and dreamy melodies he put his Castle in Spain—his great house full of music and flowers and bowing servants, in the midst of which would walk his mother in a silken gown of blue, wearing a chain of gold and diamonds about her neck.

CHAPTER 2

The town of Gaylordville prided itself on its victory when it saw the scowling band of gypsies break camp and disappear over the top of the hill. For some weeks the gypsies had occupied the little clearing just off the main road—too many weeks, the town authorities said. It was not sanitary, nor safe, they declared, and they openly laid at the gypsies' door several petty thefts that had occurred. But scarcely had Gaylordville drawn its long breath of relief, when it suddenly awoke to the fact that its troubles were by no means over—the gypsies were not gone, after all. There still remained a sick woman and a nine-year-old boy. Two days after the band of gypsies dropped out of sight behind the hill, there appeared on the Gaylordville streets a slender, lean-faced boy with somber eyes and hair that hung in curls of blackness all about his ears and neck. In his hand was a violin, and before one of the houses on a noisy street he stopped and began to play.

He had played scarcely a dozen notes when at the house door appeared a woman with an angry frown on her face, and with an upraised hand to send the boy about his business. The hand, however, fell impotently at her side and the frown disappeared from her face, while in the doorway the woman stood motionless, listening.

From all directions hurried a swarm of men, women, and children, jeering, pushing, and gleefully shrieking, "Gee, look at the kid with the fiddle!" But almost at once the shouts died into silence, and only the rise and fall of a curiously weird melody broke the hush. Then the boy stopped playing and smiled. The next moment he stood, cap in hand, before the woman in the doorway.

The woman started as if awakening from sleep. The frown

returned to her brow. "Ho, so you want money, do ye?" she snapped. "Well, who are you, anyhow? Where do you come from?"

"I'm Marco Ferdinando Bonelli, ma'am," bowed the boy, "and I come from over the hills and far away."

"Well, you can go back over the hills and far away, then, for all I care," retorted the woman, but a jeering voice from the crowd interposed.

"Why, it's Bonesy—Bonesy, the gypsy kid!"

The boy turned angrily. His cheeks burned red, and his eyes blazed with a fire that told of ancestors who were wont to fight their battles to the finish.

"Who called me Bonesy?" he demanded.

In the startled hush that answered, the woman jerked him about with a relentless hand. "See here, boy, what's the meaning of this? Why did you come back? Where are your folks?"

"I didn't come back. I was left."

"Left!"

"Yes, with Mumsey." A sudden remembrance seemed to come to the boy, and with a complete change of manner he once more held out his cap. "She's sick. It's for her I'm playin'. Haven't you got just—a penny?" he begged, tremblingly.

"No, I haven't," snapped the woman, "and if I had I shouldn't give it to the likes of you. Be gone with ye!" And the Widow Martin retreated into the house and banged the door behind her.

The Widow Martin was angry. Born upon a New Hampshire farm, and thrust by an unkind fate into a Pennsylvania mining town, she had all the New England woman's hatred of dirt, disorder, and "shiftlessness." Ten years among the Slavs, Poles, Swedes, Italians, and Portuguese all about her, moreover, had only added to her original hatred of "fureigners." That a "dirty little gypsy tramp" should presume to ask her aid was intolerable, and still more unbearable was the thought that she had so far forgotten herself as to stand and listen to his playing. But even as she frowned with anger, an echo of the witchery of that music swept over her, and involuntarily she crept to the window to see what had become of the player.

The boy was confronting the crowd, holding the violin behind his back. His face was white, and curiously set, but he received in silence the catcalls and yells of "Bonesy" from the jeering men and boys.

With an angry exclamation, the Widow Martin ran to her door and jerked it open. It had been her intention to disperse the crowd with no gentle command, but she had scarcely appeared on the doorstep when she found herself, to her dumbfounded amazement, holding a violin in her hands, while the boy—its recent guardian—was making so vigorous a use of his strong little fists that the jeers were rapidly giving place to howls of pain and rage. For a dazed minute the Widow Martin watched in silence the extraordinary sight of one small boy trying to put to silence a score of antagonists; then she dashed into the crowd, caught young Marco Ferdinando Bonelli by the collar of his blouse and dragged him into the house. Once there, she shut the door, dropped the boy into a chair, and placed the violin onto the table.

"Well, young man, this is a pretty how-d'ye-do," she said sternly.

The boy did not answer. He did not, indeed, seem to hear her. He struggled to his feet and hurried to the table, examining with anxious eyes and tender fingers the violin. Then, with a relieved sigh, he turned a beaming face on the woman.

"Thank you, ma'am—and it didn't even get scratched!" he exulted. "You were good to come and hold it for me. I was wonderin' what to do with it when you hove in sight. But I guess we fixed them all right, didn't we?"

"We! We!" gasped the Widow Martin, almost dumb at this

calm inclusion of herself in the recent fray, but the boy went on unconcernedly.

"And now, if you don't mind, I'll go. As long as you don't have anything for Mumsey, why, I must go find somebody who does, you know," he smiled cheerfully, tucking the violin under his arm.

"But what—how?" the Widow Martin stumbled over her words and came to a dazed pause. She had brought this boy into the house to give him a sound lecture. She found herself now in the uncomfortable position of one who has somehow been weighed and found wanting. "See here, boy, where is your mother?" she finished sharply.

"In the tent where they left her."

"Left her! And her sick?"

"Yessum, ma'am." The boy hesitated, then drew himself to his full height. "I didn't leave her!"

Something came into the Widow Martin's throat—a most extraordinary something that made her choke and catch her breath. She rose hurriedly and went into the next room. When she came back, she thrust a dingy ten-cent piece into the boy's hand.

"Here, now go—quick!" she commanded crossly, to hide that same something in her throat which was still there, and which forbade her voice to be steady. "Go—and don't you come back. I don't like boys, nor tramps, nor gypsies!" she flung out as she opened wide the door.

"Thank you, ma'am," joyfully beamed the boy, who seemed to be conscious of nothing but the bit of money in his hand. "Goodbye!" And he marched cheerfully through the open doorway.

It was not long before all Gaylordville knew of the boy and the sick woman whom the gypsies had left in the clearing, and all Gaylordville was disturbed. The woman was undeniably very ill, though she herself insisted that she was getting better fast and would soon be able to follow her friends, who, she said, were waiting for her a few miles farther on. Just what to do with her, the town authorities did not know. So far as air and isolation were concerned, she was best off where she was, and there really seemed to be no other place for her. The doctors declared, too, that the outdoor treatment was just what she needed, though at the same time they shook their heads gravely and prophesied that she would not long need anything. So the town authorities contented themselves by seeing that a nurse was sent to look after her wants and that curious idlers were kept away from her tent. Beyond that they gave themselves little concern.

It came to be a very common thing to see the boy about the Gaylordville streets during the days that followed, and everywhere with him was the violin. The hoots and jeers were fewer now—the impression made by his small brown fists had evidently not been forgotten. Sometimes he picked up a coin or two from a generous woman or child, but always his music brought to his side an attentive, if not an enthusiastic, group of listeners.

In Marco's own estimation, he was taking care of his mother, and never was he so pleased as when a bun or a bit of fruit he had bought for her would bring a smile to her eyes. He still sat with her in the twilight and talked of the beautiful days to come, and his violin still softly whispered of the fine new house with its bowing servants among whom she would walk in the silken gown of blue. The little mother, however, no longer sat at the door of the tent but lay back on her cot, white-faced—except for the treacherous roses—and panting for breath after the cruel cough. She said, however, that she was only tired and that she was very sure she would soon be well.

CHAPTER 3

There came a day when Marco Ferdinando Bonelli did not appear in the Gaylordville streets. He was back in the little gray tent, crying—alone.

Just what to do with Marco, Gaylordville did not know. There was no orphan asylum, no foundlings' home. There was little in Gaylordville but the mines and the silk mills. And the people were poor. Marco himself said that he would go and find his sister. He wanted Flossie, anyway. She was the only one that would understand, he said—she and the violin. But to this Gaylordville objected. It had been six weeks since the gypsies went away, and to send a nine-year-old boy afoot and alone after them was not to be thought of for an instant. Somewhere in the stunted, warped, coal-begrimed heart of Gaylordville, the little motherless boy had found a tender spot. At least, Gaylordville in a way claimed him and bestirred itself as to his welfare.

It was just here that a most extraordinary thing occurred: the Widow Martin came forward and said that she would take the boy; and with a puzzled but relieved sigh, Gaylordville promptly handed over to her Marco Ferdinando Bonelli and said that she was welcome to him.

The Widow Martin already had four mouths to feed besides her own, and for a woman who did not like "boys, nor tramps, nor gypsies," her action was certainly surprising. But there had been many a time during the last few weeks that the boy had stopped before her door and played, and though the music seldom brought her to the sight of the player, yet some of its old witchery must have entered her soul. For never was she far from a half-opened door or window, where she would stand behind sheltering curtain or blind until the last strain had died into silence far down the street.

To Marco himself this invitation of the Widow Martin's was not strange in the least. The Widow Martin was his good friend. Was it not she who had come to his assistance and enabled him to fight that jeering mob of boys? And was it not she who had given him his first coin for his mother? To be sure, it was. And to the Widow Martin's he went.

"It won't be for long, anyhow," he told her, confidently. "I'm going to play my fiddle and earn lots of money. Part of it I'll pay to you for my board and keep, and the rest I'll save to find Flossie with. You know I'm going to find Flossie first thing, right away."

It was on a warm July evening that Marco was introduced to his new home. The Widow Martin's family were at supper—if supper it might be called—those scraps and odds and ends of bread and meat and boiled potatoes. As for the family: first there was the Widow Martin herself, tall, gaunt, and somber-eyed; then there were Benny, fourteen; Susie, twelve; and Johnny, who was just past ten; and Grandpa Joe, who was—indeed, nobody knew how old. He looked to be a hundred.

To the lonely little lad who had been crying his heart out in the silent, empty tent, this group looked very inviting; and with a long sigh, he mentally took the entire family to his heart.

"I'm glad I've come," he said aloud, with a wistful smile. "I'm awful glad I've come."

Marco began work in earnest the next morning. In this he was not alone, for all the Martins—except the widow—marched sturdily off to work, too, the next morning—though with them it was not the beginning; even little Johnny had already been at work some months.

Benny was inside the mine—a "door tender." The law, it is true, said that Benny should not work underground in an anthracite mine until he was sixteen, but the law was of small consequence to

Benny or to Benny's mother. Benny could get four whole dollars and a half a week tending door, and that four dollars and a half was needed. Besides, as for the law—did he not have a certificate swearing that he was past sixteen? Certainly he did. Both Benny and Benny's mother were much too wary to be caught without that. And Benny knew how old he was, too, when people—interfering, inquisitive people—asked his age. He was "past sixteen" always—and he had been for a year.

Johnny was a "breaker-boy." His work was in the huge building that towered above the shaft through which the cars of coal were hoisted from that pit of blackness hundreds of feet below. Johnny had wanted to go down into that pit to work. Johnny was ambitious—or he had been when he first went to work. But even he knew that his dwarfed little body would hardly answer for the "past sixteen" certificate; it was as much as he could do to obtain the one that would swear he was "past fourteen" and thus eligible to the position of "breaker-boy." Johnny was not ambitious now. Nine hours a day of bending over a grinding stream of coal in the dust and roar of the coal-breaker is not conducive to the increase of ambition, and Johnny was becoming more dull-eyed and stoop-shouldered every day. Still he worked, and worked well, and every week a portion of the pittance he earned went to swell the fund in the tin coffee-pot on the top shelf of Mother's closet.

All the family knew of that coffee-pot—the wonderful coffee-pot which held the money that would one day take them all away from the mines and drop them on the green hillsides of the New Hampshire town where Mother was born—and each of the family, except Grandpa Joe, contributed every week, if possible, a coin to the coffee-pot's wealth. Grandpa Joe—Grandpa Joe did not earn much anyway, and what he did earn went for drink.

Grandpa Joe was the late Bill Martin's father, and he was a breaker "boy," too, now. Grandpa Joe had been "mighty lucky," so the men said. In all the long fifty years of his work in mines, neither powder blast nor firedamp had laid him low, nor had falling rock or a broken rope taken life or limb. He was gray and bent and shaken; but he was alive, and he could work; and he did work—beside his ten-year-old grandson in the coal-breaker. And the cycle of one more miner's life was almost complete.

As for Susie—Susie was a girl and "no good" for the mines. There had been a time, indeed, when girls in Gaylordville were at a discount, but that time was not now. Some men had noted the superfluous girls in mining towns and had looked out for them— and incidentally for themselves. Hence to Gaylordville had come the silk mills, the beneficent silk mills which could employ any number of girls, sixteen years old, fifteen, fourteen, even younger— much younger; for, as in the case of the boys in the coal-breaker, Pennsylvania girls had to be fourteen—only on paper. And Susie was fourteen—on paper; so Susie worked in the mills.

The Widow Martin worked there too, when it was possible; though her daily task of preparing for her family something to eat and something to wear was no small thing. Still, there was that hoard in the coffee-pot and the dear use to which it was one day to be put. But it grew so slowly—so woefully slowly! Sometimes it seemed as if its purpose would never be accomplished. To the Widow Martin, however, it was always something for which to live. There was always in the future that blessed day when she with her children would leave the squat, coal-begrimed shanties with their swarms of jabbering foreigners and look once more on the green hills of her childhood. And yet, in the face of all these hopes and struggles, she had taken into her home one more to feed and clothe—the little Marco Ferdinando Bonelli, of the gypsy camp.

CHAPTER 4

Marco, with his violin under his arm, went forth very bravely that first day and began to play in the streets. But Marco, the little tramp boy to whom the Widow Martin had given a home, was to Gaylordville a very different being from Marco, the mysterious little stranger earning money for his sick mother in the gypsy camp; and before many days had passed, Marco himself found this out, though he could not have put it into words. He knew only that the faces into which he looked were indifferent now, if not actually hostile; and he realized that his little cap seldom showed anything richer than a copper cent or two when it had gone the rounds of the crowd.

Perhaps, though the boy did not know it, the music was different. It no longer carried quite the joy and triumph that it had before; it no longer sang of woods and flowers and tumbling brooks and of joyous days to come. Instead, there crept into it something of the gloom of the blackened hills and the waste all about him, and something of the sob of a lonely child in a tent all alone in the clearing. Whatever it was, his playing met with a response that was anything but encouraging, and night after night, Marco went home with a heart that ached as sorely as did his little brown feet.

How, pray, he asked himself, was he to pay for his "board and keep," to say nothing of saving money to help him find his sister? As if five cents a day could do that! He looked with envy upon Benny and Johnny with their jingling coins; and once he went without his supper, only to stumble downstairs in the night to look for a crust of bread because he was so hungry he could not sleep. He found out, too, one day, about the tin coffee-pot and the hopes it carried, and after that he was more miserable than ever. His music that day was only a minor wail, like the cry of a lost dog in the desert, and two women sent him away from their front door with a shiver and an angry word.

It was then that Marco determined that something must be done. After some deliberation he summoned ten-year-old Johnny to his aid.

"I'm going to work," he announced decisively. "I'm going to begin with you tomorrow mornin.'"

"Ye can't! What's eatin' ye? You got to be fourteen."

"Fourteen!" Marco fairly screamed the words. "Why, I'm only nine and a half.

Again Johnny grinned. "Aren't you the guy to own it up!" he chuckled.

Marco frowned and doubled up his ready little fist, whereat Johnny shrugged his shoulders and hastened to make amends.

"Ho! What's eatin' ye? You can be fourteen, same as I am. I sold a paper to the squire for a quarter, and so can you."

Marco sighed his relief, but his eyes were dazed, and Johnny proceeded to explain.

"You don't have to be fourteen; you just got to say your fourteen. See? Say it now." And he struck a pompous attitude. "How old be you, Marco Ferdinando Bonelli—Bonesy?" he demanded.

For once Marco forgave the hated "Bonesy." He was too absorbed to take offense. He hesitated, then blurted it out in one shout of triumph. "I'm four—teen!"

"Right you are!" crowed Johnny, highly pleased with his pupil. "Now—got a quarter?"

Marco considered. Very slowly he reached into his pocket and produced a half of a red bandanna handkerchief tied into a series of hard knots, evidently the safeguard of some treasure. A minute later the treasure lay in his lap: a five-cent piece and fourteen copper cents.

"I only have nineteen cents," he choked, after a feverish counting of his wealth.

"Ho!" shrugged Johnny, diving into his trousers pockets and pulling both of them wrong side out. There tumbled into view a string, two nails, an odd-shaped bit of coal, a cigarette stump, a curious piece of slate, three copper cents, and one nickel. "Here, I can tend to that," he cried, picking out the nickel and one cent and airily tossing them into Marco's lap. "Now, how old be ye?"

"Fourteen!" shrieked Marco, leaping to his feet and executing a dance of triumph, keeping time with the clinking coins in the bandanna handkerchief which he had turned into a tambourine.

It was a very simple matter after that. The Widow Martin was more than willing that Marco should go to work in the coal-breaker; she had, indeed, been seriously thinking of proposing it herself. The certificate, too, was easily secured, and in due time Marco also had "a paper off the squire" which swore that he was past fourteen.

There remained then only the task of obtaining the employment itself, and there was not much doubt that there would be found to be plenty of room in the huge black coal-breaker for one more small boy.

CHAPTER 5

A new boy was always a source of more or less interest to his fellow workers in the coal-breaker. Experience likes to gloat over inexperience and chuckle at its mistakes, and ten-year-old boys are not the only ones that enjoy making a display of easy proficiency before the eyes of dazed ignorance.

In the case of Marco, the Gaylordville boys found a rich treat. It was not every day that there was introduced into their midst a boy whose home had been the green hills bounded only by the far-reaching sky and whose will had known almost no restraint in all the nine years of his life. Marco shrank from the roar of the machinery and the grinding sweep of the coal down the chutes, and he blinked at the smoky lamps gleaming from the caps of the boys. He choked and sneezed at the clouds of dust and felt his way gingerly to the little board laid across the trough where he was to begin his work. The boys jeered and grinned and thrust their blackened little faces forward with shouts of:

"Hi, there! If it isn't Bonesy, the fiddlin' kid! Say, give us a tune!"

Marco scowled and doubled up his fists threateningly, but he changed his tactics as he suddenly remembered his new dignity.

"Ho! I'm going to work. What's eatin' ye?" he scoffed airily, borrowing Johnny's pet phrase with shameless ease.

And Marco did go to work. It was not long before he learned just how to sit on the little board across the chute and just how to pick the rock and slate and "bony" from the coal that slid down the trough between his feet. It was not long, also, before his back began to ache and ache as if a dozen gimlets were boring through it, and it was not long before his little brown fingers showed scarlet tips where the sharp stone and slate had cut through the skin. He learned then what "red tops" meant.

There were three other new boys working near him, and they, too, had bleeding fingertips—and they, too, were the object of jeers and gibes because of their "blooming red tops."

Marco winced and quivered under both pain and ridicule, and in secret he sometimes cried, but he did not falter nor turn back. Day after day he trudged to the coal-breaker and took up his work in the deafening roar and the blinding dust. Day after day his back grew more lame and his arms more weary, and night after night he went home so tired that he could only throw himself down on his cot and just reach out and touch his violin. He could not have played, even if he had possessed the strength. His smarting, swollen fingers would not have allowed it.

In the coal-breaker his face became grimier, and his nose and throat became more and more choked with dust. Most keenly he missed the fresh air and the sunshine, and he longed—with an overwhelming hatred of dust and dirt—for one day in the green, quiet woods or under the wide blue sky. He rebelled, too, very bitterly against the discipline of the breaker-boss, and he remembered with scalding tears the gentle touch of his mother's hand on his hair.

Yet in the face of all this, Marco was, in a way, happy. He was earning sixty cents a day, and sixty cents is a good deal when one has tramped the streets a whole week and gained only fourteen copper cents and one nickel!

Half of this sixty cents a day Marco paid to Widow Martin for his board; the other half he tied up in the bandanna handkerchief against the day when he should go in search of Flossie. There were times, it is true, when he abstracted from this hoard a penny or a nickel and slipped it into Widow Martin's hand for the coffee-pot on the closet shelf. He saw no reason why he, as well as the others, should not contribute toward that fund, particularly as he himself knew so well what it meant to long for green fields and blue skies.

Marco had been a breaker-boy some weeks when one day the miners and their families were thrown into unusual excitement. A new mine inspector had made his appearance, and there were wild rumors that he meant to make a thorough overhauling of matters and things, particularly in regard to reported open violations of the Child Labor Law, concerning which there had been much recent agitation.

Marco was frightened. His sixty cents a day was very dear to him, and, moreover, a "raise" was confidently expected. His fingers were getting hardened, and he could work more rapidly. Marco was more anxious than ever for money now. He was growing homesick for Flossie and freedom, and he knew he could not obtain either without money. So anxious was he, indeed, that he had even seriously thought lately of suggesting to the Widow Martin that he pay only twenty cents a day for his board and go without his noon meal, so that the resulting ten cents might help to swell the fund in the bandanna handkerchief. And yet, here now was to be the end of all his scheming: a most cruel man who would take from him his entire income—his whole sixty cents a day!

"Shucks! Don't you worry," comforted Benny airily, to whom Marco confessed his fears. "It's dead easy. The boss'll fix it. 'Sides, if the 'spector does spot you, what of it? Just hold up your chin, and keep your head. You've got your paper, and you're fourteen. Don't the paper prove it, and aren't you telling him so? How's he going to get 'round that, I sh'd like to know!"

"Yes, but I thought—"

"Then don't think anything," interrupted Benny. "Just talk. Why, look a-here," he went on, waxing confidential, "They were 'most onter us nippers down below the last time, and did the boss get scared? Not much. He just chucked us little fellers out of sight behind the gob and put some of the drivers on to our job. When the Great Mogul gets along, there was nothing going on our way at all; and with his head in the air, he shoved right along past where we was laughin' fit to split. That's the last we have seen of him. Ho!

Who's 'fraid? It's just dead easy, I say!"

It did, indeed, prove to be "dead easy," as Benny had said. The Gaylordville mine was only one of a score that the inspector had on his list, and he naturally could not spend all his time in the eighty-odd miles of headings and gangways of this one mine. Neither could he be supposed to dispute successfully the ages of some two hundred boys who were like the proverbial eel for slipping out of his grasp, and who, if finally cornered, were vociferously, triumphantly—and legally—of the proper age. Then, too, looking for violations of the Child Labor Law was not the only duty of the inspector. He must be on the watch for dangerous overhanging slate, and for gas, and he must be ready to report any defects in the timbering or in the ventilation. The inspector, certainly, had little spare time on his hands to devote to boys.

Some changes were made, it is true. A few boys were discharged, and many more disappeared from their accustomed places for a short time. There were sharp words, accusations, warnings, and threats of trouble in the near future. Then the mine inspector went away.

Marco drew a long breath of relief. He still had his sixty cents a day and the "raise" in prospect. He had been "spotted," to be sure, and had been made to show his certificate, but he had closely followed Benny's instructions and had come out unharmed, though the mine inspector had frowned, had said a bad word under his breath, and had shown indications of pursuing the subject further when the breaker-boss had contrived to attract his attention to something much more serious. Marco had gladly taken the opportunity then to slip away.

CHAPTER 6

Marco had been at work just six weeks when one morning he awoke so ill that he could not stand on his feet. For some days the Widow Martin dosed him conscientiously and impartially with one after another of the various medicines in her cupboard; then, meeting with results that could scarcely be called successful, she sent for the doctor.

The doctor looked grave. He had seen something of the sick woman left in the gypsy tent long weeks before, and he knew what Marco had to fight in the way of inherited frailness of constitution, to say nothing of possible disease. In a week, however, he had Marco on his feet, but he distinctly forbade any more work in the coal-breaker for some months to come. He prescribed fresh air and sunshine, and plenty of them—in short, an outdoor life. The coal-breaker was not to be thought of.

It was a grievous blow to Marco. Not only was his sixty cents a day a thing of the past, but the treasured little hoard in the bandanna handkerchief must go now to pay the Widow Martin for the past two weeks' board.

On the hill far above the coal-breaker, Marco tried to figure it out one Sunday afternoon with Johnny to help him.

After all, Johnny was not much help. Johnny's schooling was a thing of shreds and patches—a thing of evening classes in a stuffy room after a long day's work, when boys—little boys eight and nine and ten years old—cannot keep awake, much less learn the meaning of strange hieroglyphics on a tattered, much-thumbed page.

Johnny's employer, the great mine-king (though Johnny did

not know it), thought a great deal of education. In a distant city, an imposing college building bore his name, and the world rang with acclamations of this great man who so generously donated large sums yearly to the maintenance of this admirable institution. Perhaps Johnny himself might be said to have a hand in this good work. Certainly his long days of labor at four dollars and a half a week added its mite to the great whole that made possible the fortune, which in turn made possible the college. As for his own education—Johnny attended night-school on occasional winter evenings, when his work left him strength to get there. No, certainly Johnny could not be of much help to Marco.

Marco had been taught by his mother. He could read and write, and he said he could "figure some." At all events, he produced paper and pencil and began to jot down the items.

"It has been three weeks since I paid your ma" he began, dolefully, "and I pay her a dollar and eighty cents a week. How much is three times a dollar and eighty cents?"

"Give it up," retorted Johnny, promptly.

"Well, how do you spell 'owe'?"

"Don't spell it. What's eatin' ye?"

"Yes, but if you do?"

"Ye got me! Why, isn't 'O' good enough—just the letter 'O'?"

"Guess it is," murmured Marco, abstractedly.

There was a long pause. Marco was covering the wrong side of his paper with laboriously-made figures and was making visible use of his lips and his fingers for counting.

"Johnny, it's five whole dollars and forty cents!" he groaned at last. "Gee! Don't it count up when it isn't paid right along! Five dollars and forty cents!"

"Maybe Ma'll chuck out the forty cents," suggested Johnny,

hopefully. "Ye haven't eaten much lately, you know."

"But there's the doctor—and doctors cost awful!" wailed Marco.

"Gee, so they does," murmured Johnny. "I forgot the pill-peddler."

"He came three times, and he said it was a dollar a time for me; I asked him. And that would make three dollars more." There was another long pause while Marco worked again with his pencil; then there was a shriek of dismay. "Johnny, it's eight dollars and forty cents! Why, Johnny, there won't be nothin' left to find Flossie with!"

Johnny was properly sympathetic, but he was also hopeful. There might be more in the bandanna handkerchief than Marco thought. He suggested that they immediately go down to the house and find out. And to the house they went as fast as their eager little legs could carry them.

Ten minutes later the boys were looking into each other's faces in blank dismay—the bandanna handkerchief with its treasure was nowhere to be found.

There was at once the wildest confusion. All the Martins except Grandpa Joe were at home, and all gathered around Marco with expressions of deepest concern. No one had seen it; no one knew anything about it. Marco himself had not seen it since the night before, when he had put it back under the loose board in the corner of the room which he shared with Johnny and Benny. It was gone, certainly, probably stolen. But as for suspecting any one of the Martin family of the theft, Marco never so much as thought of it.

Widow Martin, however, did think of it. A sickening fear clutched at her heart as she remembered that she had seen her father-in-law near the boys' room only that morning. She said nothing to Marco, but the fear became a conviction when that night word was brought to the Martin cottage that the old man had "a jag on to beat the band," and was "treatin' right and left." Marco did not hear this. He had gone to bed and had sobbed himself to sleep.

Marco was astir early the next morning. The four walls of his room seemed to stifle him. There was nothing but the hills and the wide dome of the sky that could comfort him today—that could make life even endurable. Scarcely swallowing a morsel of the breakfast that the Widow Martin pressed upon him, he tucked his violin under his arm and fled from the house.

Marco had played a good deal during the last few days. He had even tried to go back to his street-playing for money. But today he hurried through the town without pausing until he came to the road that led by the clearing where had been the gypsy camp. Then he threw himself down on the grass beside the road to rest and to think.

Something must be done. He owed for three weeks' board and for three doctor's visits, and he had no money to pay. More than that, he could not earn the money now, and he had lost every cent that he had saved to use in his search for Flossie.

With mournful eyes he followed the sweep of the road as it led to the top of the hill and dropped out of sight on the other side. Somewhere over there was Flossie; he knew that. And Flossie was waiting for Mother, the mother who could never come now. And he—perhaps he, too, would never come. It looked, certainly, as if he would not until he was old and gray—and rich. And Marco pictured himself as he would be then, staff in hand and searching the wide world over for Flossie. It was not an unpleasant picture, after all; for money jingled in his pockets, and Flossie was in sight, waiting and smiling to receive him. Marco was quite delighting in it, indeed, when a strain of music from the door of a house some distance behind him caused him to turn quickly.

He recollected then that it had been coming nearer and nearer—that music. He saw now what had produced it—a hand-organ. He watched until the organ-grinder stopped turning the crank and went to receive something from the woman in the doorway. It seemed to be a sandwich or a piece of pie, which the man took in his fingers and ate, picking up his organ afterward and coming up the road toward where Marco was sitting. He did not stop nor glance up, but plodded on and on up the road that led to the top of the hill.

For one, two, three minutes Marco watched the man with eyes that grew moment by moment more wistful; then, giving a sudden exclamation, he sprang to his feet and hurried after him.

"Look a-here—say—Mister, where you goin'?" he called.

The man turned slowly. His eyes looked out from under a heavy fringe of black, and his face showed lines that were not carved by laughter and good temper. He gave a guttural grunt, which Marco cheerfully accepted as being interrogatory.

"I say, where are you goin'?" he repeated in a louder tone. "Maybe I could go, too. Would you take me?"

"Humph!" The anger was unmistakable this time, even to Marco. The man turned and began to plod up the hill.

"But, say, Mister—please," begged Marco, his eager little feet keeping him abreast of the organ.

The man shook his head. "No want-a da kid," he growled over his shoulder.

"But I won't bother a mite," urged the boy. "It's my sister—I want to find her, and you're going just where she did, right up over that hill."

Again the man shook his head. This time Marco could not understand what he said, but that it was not encouraging was most painfully evident. Marco, however, was not of the sort that is easily repressed. He still ran beside the organ, still smiled cheerfully, and still pleaded his cause.

"And I can play, too, Mister," he cried. "I can earn money. Listen!" And with fingers trembling with eagerness, he lifted the violin to position and drew the bow across the strings. The man stopped abruptly. Very slowly he turned, brought his organ to the ground, and rested his elbows upon it. Across his countenance swept interest, wonder, and amazement, while all about him rippled the runs and trills and rollicking melodies by which Marco was endeavoring to prove that he could "play." Then gradually into the man's face crept a slow cunning. His eyes narrowed until they were mere slits, but they never swerved from their now exulting scrutiny of the boy's rapt face and long, slender fingers.

"There!" breathed Marco at last, lowering his violin and quiveringly awaiting the verdict.

"Humph!" grunted the man. "Who learn-a you like that?"

"Mumsey. But she said I did better 'n her. Granddad played, too, and she says I play more like him," declared the boy proudly. "He was a big one. He played in concerts, and 'fore kings and queens, and I'm going to, too."

"Humph!" The man lowered his eyes. His next words were spoken indifferently, but with peculiar distinctness. "What you call-a her—your 'mumsey'—you live-a together?"

Marco shook his head. His eyes filled, and his chin quivered.

"She's dead. That's just it, you see. They've all gone—my folks—and I want to find 'em. I want Flossie, my sister."

The man stirred suddenly. He lifted his head and showed a gleaming row of white teeth in a beguiling smile.

"I take-a you. Come—we go!" he said, holding out his hand. "We find a your secotaire!"

Marco gave a joyous skip, though he did not take the proffered hand.

"But you'll have to wait just a little, Mister," he cried excitedly. "There's some things I've got to get first. It won't take but a jiffy. Wait here—I'll come!" He turned to run, but a sharp word from the man brought him right about face in surprise. The man was smiling, however, when he met Marco's eyes, and his voice when he next spoke was gentleness itself.

"Maybe they not let-a you come back," he suggested softly.

Marco hesitated. It was true. Perhaps they would not let him come back. He remembered now that his plan of going to find his sister had been frowned upon from the first. To be sure, he was going alone then, while now he had this good kind man to guide him, and that might make a difference in the way they looked at the matter. Still, it would be better, perhaps, to be on the safe side. He certainly could not afford to let this chance slip through his fingers.

"I reckon maybe I—won't—tell 'em—where I'm goin'," he said aloud, slowly; and in the quick smile and grunt of approval that the man gave, Marco read that his decision was a wise one.

Marco found only the Widow Martin at home, and he managed to slip into the house and up to the boys' room without attracting her attention. There were but few things, after all, that he possessed, and these were mostly keepsakes of his mother's: a little green-covered book, a watch, a ring, and a locket containing the likeness of a man with somber dark eyes very like Marco's own. These trinkets, together with a few odds and ends of clothing that had been given to Marco since he came to Gaylordville, formed a bundle that was not too large for a small boy's arms to carry in addition to the violin in its case.

Only one thing troubled Marco—the money that he owed the good Widow Martin for his three weeks' board and for the doctor's visits. It did not seem right to slink off like this without a word. Ever since Marco could remember, this one thing had been instilled into him: what he could not pay for he must not have. As he looked back at it now, he knew that the very reason that his mother so specially emphasized this point was because that all about him in his gypsy life he saw so many cases of having—and not paying.

So it was the debt that troubled him, and it was the debt that nearly sent him to the Widow Martin with the frank statement that he was going away, but that he would come back someday and "pay up." More potent than all this, however, was the fear that such a confession would end in the defeat of all his schemes; so, after some hesitation, Marco wrote a few words on a scrap of paper and pinned it to his pillow. Then he stole from the house and ran swiftly down the street.

Long hours afterward the Widow Martin, coming into the boys' room, found this on Marco's bed:

"Deer Mis Widder Martin. I O your 5 dollars and 40 cents and for the Doctor 3 times. I will pay up sum day. Good by. Marco Ferdinando Bonelli."

CHAPTER 7

It was a rude awakening for Marco. He had pictured a joyous, easy pilgrimage over wooded hills and through sleepy villages, with a good, kind man to help him find his sister. He experienced something quite different.

The "joyous, easy pilgrimage" became a forced march, on which his tired little legs were compelled to keep up with the strides of a man accustomed to walking miles every day; and the "wooded hills" and "sleepy villages" became long stretches of dust-white road leading to villages that were very much awake to the undesirability of harboring a vagabond organ-grinder and a shabby small boy. It rained, too, very frequently, and the wide blue sky was then only a chill expanse of misty gray.

Nor was the "good, kind man" the same. Marco had not passed two days with the organ-grinder before he learned this. By that time there was not even a semblance of kindness in the man's voice or manner; and Marco found himself with a traveling companion whose only conversation consisted of a sharp command or a surly grunt. Marco learned something else, too—something that puzzled him very much: the man had forgotten almost everything he knew about English. He could not speak it nor understand it—except very occasionally; and yet, as Marco well remembered, they had experienced no trouble at all in making themselves clear to each other on that first day.

The man knew enough now, to be sure, to tell Marco when to play his violin and when to pass his cap for the money. But afterward, when Marco wanted some of that money for a trifling purchase at a village store, he could not seem to make the man understand at all what he meant, and he was obliged to go without it. The man carried the money, of course. He had made it very plain to Marco that it was not safe for a small boy to have any of it; and Marco, remembering the lost bandanna handkerchief, had readily agreed with him.

There was another thing, too, that the man seemed strangely to have forgotten—the very reason for Marco's presence. From the first, Marco had talked of Flossie. It had almost seemed to him, indeed, that from the top of the hill he would see the gypsy tents where she would be; and it was a keen disappointment to him to find on the other side of the hill only a long, straight road leading to the top of still another hill. He had said little at the time, but when three days had gone by and there was still no sign of the longed-for tents, he asked the man what it meant, explaining that the gypsies had promised to wait not far away for his mother to come to them and that he knew that they intended to camp somewhere in that vicinity all summer.

The man, however, did not understand. He seemed to have forgotten all about Flossie and the search. He listened to Marco's carefully worded explanation with an angry scowl, and he replied with only a grunt and a few sharp words in a language Marco did not understand—Marco knew little but English, so jealously had his mother kept him to herself and to her own language.

If the man had forgotten Flossie, however, Marco had not; day after day his eyes swept the landscape for some glimpse of a tent. He had almost given up hope when, one day, he saw them—those gray-white tents in a field down the road ahead.

With a joyful leap he sprang forward and tugged at the organ-grinder's coat.

"It's Flossie—it's my folks—I've found them!" he shouted excitedly. "Come—let's hurry!"

The organ-grinder frowned and shook his head. He did not appear to know what Marco was talking about, and he jerked himself away from the boy's touch with an angry word. Worse yet, he turned off at a crossroad before he came to the tents, and insisted that this was the way they must go.

"But I can't—I mustn't! Don't you see?" cried Marco, frantically. "It's Flossie—I'm going to her!" And he turned and ran back by himself to the other road.

With a snarl of rage, the organ-grinder hurried after him and clutched his arm.

"You come-a this way. You hear?" he growled, with an oath, and with a series of expletives that Marco could not understand. What Marco did understand, however, was the way he was dragged along the hated road that led away from those gray-white tents.

Suddenly into his mind came an illuminating thought. It was already nearly dark, and they would not go far—things might not be so hopeless, after all! So with a semblance of cheerfulness he obediently played for their supper at the first house they came to, and with a studiously contented air he laid himself down in the dilapidated shed which the organ-grinder a little later found for their night's shelter.

Marco did not go to sleep, however. That was not part of his plan. He waited until the deep breathing of the man at his side proclaimed that his guardian slept; then he picked up his violin and stole out into the moonlight. It was nearly a mile back to the field where the gray-white tents stood; but Marco's tired little feet did not falter. On and on they sped down the long white road until they came to the turn, just beyond which lay the field with the tents. Marco went more cautiously now. He had no wish to rouse the camp. He wanted to see Flossie, and only Flossie, at first. He had some questions to ask before he gave up his freedom for the gypsy camp. He could conceive of conditions that might make it preferable that he take Flossie away with him, instead of staying himself with her.

It had been a puzzle to him at first just how he was to accomplish this interview with Flossie; then in a flash had come the solution: he would play "Lost on the Ocean Wave," and she would know that he was there and would come out to find him.

"Lost on the Ocean Wave" was a plaintive little melody of Marco's own, which Flossie had loved and which she herself had named.

"It's just like the ocean, and it moans and moans," she sighed rapturously one day. "And by and by the stars come out and light up their lamps in the sky; and there isn't anything anywhere, only one little boat all alone, just like the picture in the book, and it's lost—all lost! I'm going to call it 'Lost on the Ocean Wave,' just like the picture," she declared. And after that she always asked for it by that name.

Very stealthily Marco slipped into the field and approached the tents. On the farther side a clump of bushes offered a hiding-place, and in the shadow of these he took up his position to play. That others in the camp besides Flossie might hear him, he did not doubt; but that they would associate him with the melody he did not believe. He intended, too, to stop playing the moment there was a stir of life about the tents, and he would not make himself known until the bright moonlight had told him whether it was Flossie or someone else that had been aroused. That Flossie would come if she heard him, he knew; and on this he pinned his faith.

To Marco this playing in the moonlight to charm his sister from a gypsy tent in the middle of the night did not seem unusual in the least. Neither did it seem strange to him that he should have found the camp. Always before Marco's confident eyes had been the gray-white tents; and as for the rest—since babyhood Marco had lived a dream-life that was much more real than the reality; and anything that had to do with music and moonlight and lost sisters-found was the most natural thing in the world—in Marco's world.

The music rose and swelled and died away, then rose again in a plaintive call. Marco strained eyes and ears, but there was no stir, no sound. Suddenly a hand touched his arm.

"Marco!" cried an amazed voice.

"Jake!" And Marco turned to confront a small boy who, with a caution that matched Marco's own, had crawled through the grass on the farther side of the tents and had skirted the field to reach the player's side.

"What you doin'? Where you been all this time, Marco?"

Marco tossed his head impatiently.

"Never mind that now. Where's Flossie? I want Flossie?"

Jake dropped his eyes and shifted uneasily from one foot to the other. "What do you want Flossie? Why am I not good enough?" he demanded.

"Because you aren't," retorted Marco sharply. "I want Flossie, and I'm going to have her, too!" he finished, raising his violin to his chin.

Jake put out a restraining hand.

"Sh-h! Look a-here, do you want to rout out the whole camp? 'Sides, Flossie isn't there."

"She isn't there?"

"No, she's gone."

"Gone!" In his stupefaction Marco could only repeat Jake's words. But after a moment his tongue and his wits came back, and he poured into Jake's ears a torrent of questions.

It was Jake's turn to toss his head.

"I don't know, and none of us do" he muttered sulkily. "She was here one day, and the next she wasn't. All I know is, there was a man, and he got her. Some says he was her dad, and some says he just 'dopted her. No one knows except Uncle Jake. He fixed it up with the man, and he isn't doing any talking.

"But don't you know nothing? Not where they've gone, nor

nothing?" Marco's voice shook. He was afraid he was going to cry—and to cry before Jake was unthinkable disgrace.

"To New York, maybe. Some says it was New York."

New York! Marco lifted his head suddenly. That was the name that the organ-grinder had snarled out the night before, when he had insisted on turning down the crossroad. He was going to New York. Joyfully now came Marco's decision. Without so much as a word to the amazed boy at his side, he turned and sped across the moonlit field. Five minutes later he had made the turn and was hurrying down the long white road that led to the shed where he had left the organ-grinder.

It was a very simple matter, after all, decided Marco. He had but to go with the man, and he would reach New York, and in New York was Flossie. Then he need only play "Lost on the Ocean Wave" before every house until Flossie heard and threw open the door.

CHAPTER 8

It was very cold when Marco reached New York. For days now he had been plodding through what seemed to be endless streets that led between interminable rows of houses. Marco had not supposed, indeed, that there were so many houses in the world. As for New York itself, Marco could but wonder how he was to find one particular fluffy-haired, blue-eyed little girl under all that wilderness of roofs.

In New York Marco began at once to learn many things. Strange to say, the organ-grinder's knowledge of English seemed suddenly to have come back, and he imparted several bits of information that were both startling and disconcerting. To begin with, he said that the money was all gone—spent on the way. Marco was surprised at this, for he knew that almost every day his little cap had jingled pleasantly with coins, and he thought that few of these had been needed to pay for food or lodging or the occasional "lift" given them by some obliging driver. Still the man said the money was gone, and surely the man, who had taken charge of the money from the first, must know.

Marco was grieved and disappointed. He had not known exactly what he meant to do—but there would be the money, and there would be Flossie waiting to be found. The rest seemed simple. But now that the money was gone, it was not simple at all. Marco was very much discouraged. The man, too, seemed sorry, and suggested that Marco live with him for a time, so that he might earn more money; and Marco, thinking that, after all, the man was not so unkind as he seemed, gratefully accepted the offer.

Marco discovered then that there were people in the world who lived in the most extraordinary fashion: hived in groups of four, eight, even twelve or more in a single room—and that room a loathsome thing of dirt and darkness at the top or at the bottom of some dismal house. How a man who, like the organ-grinder, knew the joy of sunny days and starlit nights out in the open, could live like this was beyond Marco's comprehension.

Marco did not like the organ-grinder's home. He did not like the dirty street and the dirtier alley that led to it; and he did not like the view from its one window—broken-hinged blinds and straggling clothes-lines festooned across a ten-foot, refuse-strewn back yard. Neither did he like the room. There was little light and no comfort in it; moreover, all the best corners were already occupied by the organ-grinder's brother and his wife with their six children. Even at that, one must climb four rickety flights of stairs to reach it and feel one's way through long dingy halls, where sometimes a drunken man lay stretched across one's path. Bad as it was, however, Marco was forced to admit that it was better than nothing; for in it one might obtain at least a respite from the terrifying rush and roar of the streets. Marco privately decided, nevertheless, that he would not long impose on the organ-grinder's kindness. As soon as sufficient money was earned, he would set out at once upon his search for Flossie.

It did not take the organ-grinder long to make his plans. Marco was to go out with Annetta, the organ-grinder's niece. Annetta could sing and dance—after a fashion of her own, and together they would pick up much money—so the organ-grinder said.

Annetta was twelve years old, pretty, pert, and self-confident; and though the musical Italian syllables rippled through her red lips like bubbling waters from a never failing spring, yet the English came, too—such English as it was —almost as rapidly. She knew the city streets at every turn and would make a most efficient guide and companion for Marco. She liked the idea, too, and she liked Marco. She began at once to lay her plans.

"Tune her up. Let's hear you play," she said to the boy.

Marco hesitated. He was tired and homesick. Not once since

he came had he touched the violin. The sordid dreariness of his surroundings had crushed out all his desire to play. It seemed to him that the violin itself would refuse to speak in the stifling atmosphere. But even as he hesitated, he realized that he must play, for in his violin lay all his hopes of escape. There was one melody, too, that he could play—one melody that would be a relief to his aching heart. The next moment he was throwing all his longing soul into the first strains of "Lost on the Ocean Wave."

For a time Annetta listened in silence, then she jerked the boy's sleeve angrily. "See here, you—cut it out! This is no funeral," she scoffed. "Give us something that is alive. You aren't going to play that kind of tune."

Marco frowned. He stopped playing instantly and drew himself stiffly erect.

"Then you needn't come with me," he retorted, decisively. "That's my sister's piece, and it's a-goin' to be played. So, there!"

Annetta stared; then she gave a gleeful laugh in recognition of a spirit as untamable as her own.

"Gee! Isn't he the nice little man now, what thinks he owns the whole block!" she chuckled. Then, with mocking meekness, she added: "Of course, if you want them to think it's a funeral, why, I'm not saying anything; and of course I didn't know your fiddle couldn't play but one tune!"

The shot went home. Marco jerked his violin into place and burst into such a swirl of runs and trills and merry little tunes that Annetta's feet could not keep to the floor, but danced about the room in a very ecstasy of joy.

"Oh, stop—stop!" she panted, dropping to the floor in a little heap. "It isn't fair to spring it like that—all to once. Say, but you—are—great!" she exulted then, with a blissful sigh.

They began to practice after that, soberly and with an eye to business. Half of Marco's "pieces" were improvisations, or little melodies of his own that he had played often enough to memorize. To all of these, Annetta had no difficulty in timing her eager little feet. But Annetta's songs were another matter. They were a curious jumble of street ballads, vaudeville jingles, and Salvation Army hymns, and they were all new to Marco. Annetta had only to sing them over a few times, however, before Marco had caught their tune and rhythm and was playing with her, now in unison, and now in harmonious thirds and sixths, which brought a delighted sparkle to Annetta's eyes.

"Gee, but you are great!" she would cry again and again. "Just wait till we get after 'em! We'll make them fork over the chink!"

CHAPTER 9

At the very beginning of their "concert tower" (as Annetta called their invasion of the city streets), Marco made one stipulation: every time they stopped to play and sing he should be allowed to play, at least once, "Lost on the Ocean Wave," otherwise he would not play at all. Much as Annetta hated the "funeral tune," she was forced to consent to its being included in their "show," and she acquiesced all the more readily when she learned the purpose of its being played.

This fantastical search for the missing Flossie by means of a familiar melody appealed to her love of adventure very strongly, yet she could not hold out much encouragement that it would be successful.

"It's all right, and I'm glad to do it," she told Marco. "But as for thinkin' it's a-goin' to fetch her—nit! Just as if we'd get to find her house in all these millions and millions of streets! Pooh! Of course we couldn't!"

Notwithstanding her misgivings, however, Annetta showed the liveliest interest on that first day when Marco began to play Flossie's piece, and she found herself looking at every door in sight really expecting to see one of them flung wide open by a fluffy-haired, blue-eyed little girl, who would fly into Marco's arms. No such little girl appeared, however, neither on that day nor the next, nor the next, until even Marco himself was near to giving up in despair, and Annetta had to turn comforter.

"Don't you fret," she soothed him. "It isn't as if there aren't heaps and heaps more streets where we haven't been yet. Besides, I said it wasn't sure we would get her for yet a while."

"Yes, I know," moaned the boy. "But, you see, Annetta, I want her—and I want her right now!"

It was not many days before Marco and Annetta had the routine of their performance well in hand. Marco played and Annetta sang and danced; then, while Annetta passed her cap for the money, Marco played alone, the brightest, liveliest music that he could think of. He would have half the children about him dancing by that time, and many were the passers-by that stopped to smile and listen, and to toss a coin, until Annetta's little cap quite sagged with wealth. So much money, indeed, did Marco and Annetta bring home that the organ-grinder was well pleased. He told Marco that he would keep his share for him where it would be safe from harm. He said that there were thieves and bad men in New York and that it would be better to have the money hidden away. And Marco, again remembering the red bandanna handkerchief, agreed.

The organ-grinder was really pleasant these days—except when he was drunk, which, after all, was not seldom. He was quite jovial, indeed, at times. He did not go out with his organ at all now, and when Marco questioned him, he only mumbled something about a "license" which Marco could not understand. The man had money to spend, however, though he did little work himself, which was a combination quite strange to his mind. But his joy was short-lived, after all, for into the paradise of his ease crept discomfort in the shape of the "school-man" who came to look for Annetta and to inquire into her prolonged absence from school.

Annetta's father was wary. So, too, was the organ-grinder. They said nothing about the street-playing and the money earned. They told of illness and even hinted at broken bones as a reason for Annetta's absence. But they told none of it very clearly, and they protested that they did not know what the school-man was talking about, most of the time. They were in the midst of the discussion when Annetta and Marco walked into the room.

The organ-grinder said a sharp word behind his teeth and attempted to thrust Marco out of sight, but it was too late. The school-man had seen him, and he began at once to question him.

It all ended as the organ-grinder knew it would end: Annetta must go back to school and with her must go the new boy, Marco, so that he might be properly examined and put where he belonged.

"But I don't want to go to school," stormed Marco, when the man had gone.

"Course not," snapped Annetta, "and no more don't I, but we got to."

"What for?"

Annetta shrugged her shoulders. "How do I know?" she sniffed.

Marco was silent. Across the room the organ-grinder and his brother in a torrent of Italian were cursing the school, the teacher, and the man who would take a child from his honest work—where he could be of some use—and set him to learning foolish things from books which would not bring in a single cent! The men were still snarling when Marco turned to Annetta with a sudden light in his eyes.

"Look a-here, say," he demanded, "there are girls, isn't there, at this school where we're goin'?"

"Sure!"

"Well, I'm goin', then. I want to go," announced the boy, with decision. "You see, it's there that Flossie'll be, sure. Flossie always did think books, with readin' and pictures in 'em, was all that she was doin'!"

In spite of Annetta's scornful protests, Marco took his violin to school with him on that first day, and great was his indignation when it was promptly taken away from him and carried to the desk. Nor was that the only source of his disappointment. School, in fact, so far as Marco was concerned, was a distinct failure, for how was he to find Flossie if he could not be allowed to go from room to room and play "Lost on the Ocean Wave"? And how was he to look for her at all if every bit of his time must be taken up with tiresome books and classes? No, certainly Marco did not like school.

School, however, was only the beginning of his troubles, as Marco soon found. His life at home—if home the dingy room might be called—grew day by day more unbearable. The organ-grinder had gone back to his grossest surliness, and Marco was forced more than once to dodge an angry blow. Food, too, became daily more scanty and unpalatable, until Marco seriously thought of running away and trying to fend for himself. Just here, however, he faced a grave question: what could he do to earn money?

The street-playing now was not the profitable thing that it had been. First of all, school took most of Marco's time, and though he had valiantly tried to improve such time as was left, he had encountered a brand-new difficulty in the shape of certain officious persons who did not like to see a ten-year-old boy and a twelve-year-old girl shivering in the December twilight, trying to earn a little money. These officious persons did not rest, indeed, until they had quite put a stop to it; and Marco found himself, as he expressed it, out of a job.

How, now, should he find Flossie, he wondered, bitterly, if "Lost on the Ocean Wave" was to be forever imprisoned in the silent violin?

CHAPTER 10

Some days before Christmas, Marco took to the streets. In the gray chill of dawn, he slipped out of the dismal room, carrying in one hand the violin and in the other all the rest of his earthly possessions.

He had no money. The night before he had asked the careful guardian of his earnings to give him what was coming to him—and he had got it—but it was not money: it was a blow, together with a snarling oath. For some time afterward, Marco had lain in his corner, smarting with pain and indignation. Then had come his decision. He would go away. He would go far away. He would travel miles and miles of those endless streets until he came to a place so very far away that those unkind people who would not let him play could not find him. There he would begin a new life. There he would play and earn money. He had done it before, he could do it again; and this time there would be no surly man to deprive him of all his wealth. He would find Flossie, too; and, like the people in story books, they would all live happy ever after. So, very stealthily, he had slipped out of the room, and in five minutes he was free, with the world before him.

For some time Marco plodded steadily onward, turning such corners as pleased his fancy; then a very insistent clamoring in the region of his stomach reminded him that breakfast, even such as the organ-grinder supplied, was better than no breakfast at all.

He stopped and hesitated. There was his violin, but was he at a distance that would make his playing safe? His judgment said no, but his stomach said yes; and his stomach, having the louder voice, won the day. Carefully depositing his bundle at his feet, he took out his violin and began to play.

The street was wide and thronged with people, and for a time he attracted scant attention. Then someone stopped to listen, followed by another and another. Marco played as if life itself depended on it. The old light came back to his eyes and the old joyous smile to his lips. Then he doffed his cap and presented its mute appeal to the nearest man in the crowd.

There was a quick response. The pennies and even a nickel or two were jingling merrily when a tall woman in black touched Marco on the shoulder.

"See here, little boy."

Marco turned swiftly. With instinctive caution he backed toward the bundle and the empty violin case that lay waiting for him a few feet away. His lips were silent, but his eyes were furtively measuring the way to the nearest corner.

"Who are you? What is your name?" continued the woman. "How does it happen that you are playing like this in the streets?"

Marco shook his head. Suddenly a sly cunning, the heritage of his recent environment, came to his eyes, and he mumbled glibly: "No speak-a da English."

"Indeed!" retorted the woman. "All the more reason, then, why you should be where you belong—in school!"

School! Marco did not wait to hear more. With a swiftness born of his terror, he caught up his belongings and made a dive for the nearest corner. Nor did he stop running until he had placed two long blocks between him and his tormentor. Then he paused for breath and to take account of stock.

His money was safe. He had twenty-two cents. More than that, he suddenly awoke to a realization that he had found a new weapon for defense—a convenient simulation of not understanding what was said to him. Not for nothing had he spent those past long weeks with the organ-grinder and his friends! Still he was frightened, and a little worried, as to his prospects. He felt tempted to cry, but he told himself that he was a man now, with a man's work to do, and that he must not be a baby.

By night, however, Marco almost wished that he were a baby; for babies—in his opinion—stood a fair chance of having a roof over their heads and a place to sleep. Often in the stuffy little room in the nights past he had longed for the stars and the open sky, but this was different. He had now the stars and the sky, to be sure, but he had also the thronging rush and roar of the streets, and he had the dread presence of the "cop," whose sharp-eyed scrutiny he had long since learned to fear. He was not hungry (ten cents of the twenty-two had attended to that), and he was not cold—the weather, fortunately, having turned strangely warm for December—but he was sleepy. It was quite midnight, however, before he found a secluded doorway to an empty house, where he finally curled himself up to sleep.

CHAPTER 11

In less than a week, Marco was forced to own that freedom was not the paradise he had pictured it. Earnings were scanty and irregular, particularly as he seemed never able to get away from the eyes of unkind people who, like the tall woman in black, questioned his playing. Whether these questioners always meant evil, Marco did not know, nor did he dare wait to find out. He always fled at once. Naturally this ever-present fear of molestation soon showed in his music, and Marco discovered that the coins tossed to him grew fewer and fewer each day. Flossie, too, had not been found, though he had played "Lost on the Ocean Wave" at least once whenever he had dared to play at all. It was colder now, with occasional flurries of snow, and Marco's thin little legs and arms shook until they were blue. Even the organ-grinder's home seemed a palace beside the doorways and hidden corners that were Marco's nightly bed; while as for the jabbering swarms of Italians—they seemed now like dear friends to the lonely little lad who had no one in all the great city to call him by name.

It was on Christmas Eve that matters came to a crisis with Marco. All day he had been tramping the streets, in a new-fallen snow, trying to earn a few cents for his supper. He carried now only the violin and its case in his hands. The extra coat and blouse that had been in his bundle he had put on over his other clothing; and the keepsakes of his mother he had stowed in his pockets with careful fingers—very dear to Marco were the watch, the ring, the locket, and the little green-covered book that had been his mother's, and not for much would he have parted with them. Everywhere about him were eager faces and hurried footsteps. Nowhere was there man, woman, or child who had time to listen to a wavering tune played by numbed fingers on a violin, and Marco had at last put up his instrument in despair.

All about him he saw the red and green of the Christmas cheer, but there was not a scarlet berry nor a tinsel star that did not seem to mock at him, and there was not a Christmas package that did not carry a pang to his lonely little heart and empty stomach. Even the newsboys and bootblacks wore a sprig of green and plied their trade with a holiday air, bringing a bitter envy to Marco's soul.

Marco was still thinking of the newsboy when he slipped into the great railroad station at Forty-second Street to warm himself. He had been there frequently of late. It was warm and light; and by not sitting too long in one seat, he had found he could easily avoid being asked embarrassing questions. Tonight it must have been the thought of the newsboys that gave him his Great Idea when the man near him left his evening paper on the seat and hurried away.

The paper was whole and clean—and instantly the Great Idea sprang into life. If he, Marco, could find other papers like that, why could he not take them out and sell them? Why could not he, too, be a newsboy? With the money thus earned he could buy more papers, and with the money from them, more, and yet more papers. Of course! It was a very simple matter, after all! And to Marco the way led straight ahead to bewildering wealth, and all on account of one discarded newspaper there at his side.

Marco began business at once. By diligent searching and watchfulness, he managed to possess himself of five papers. Then came the question of what he should do with his violin. As for taking it with him into that whirl of competition on the street—that was not to be thought of for a moment. He was looking about with anxious eyes for a safe hiding-place when his glance fell on the man behind one of the windows along the wall, who seemed to be taking in bags and bundles for people in the most obliging fashion. The man and the place looked safe, and with a sigh of relief Marco hurried toward the window. A moment later an amazed checking-clerk found a battered violin case thrust into his hands by an eager-eyed boy who stopped only to burst out:

"If ye'll please keep it, Mister, till I want it—and thank ye!" And he was gone before the man behind the counter could as much as say the word "check."

On the street Marco paused to consider. He wished to select the most advantageous position. He felt, too, the need of some instruction; and, for a few minutes, he did nothing but watch very carefully the movements of the newsboy nearest him. Then, taking up his position on a busy corner, he began work in earnest.

"Paper—paper—all about the big fire!" he shouted, dodging in and out of the crowd, and thrusting his papers under the noses of the passers-by.

He had sold just three papers when a shrill voice yelled in his ear: "Hey—you—beat it! This is my corner!" With the words came a stinging blow.

Marco did not stop to make inquiries. He dropped his papers and responded with fists and feet. He was getting much the better of his assailant when suddenly he stopped short—the boy he was pommeling was even smaller than himself and was a hunchback.

The hunchback, amazed at this sudden cessation of hostilities at the very moment of victory, stopped too and gazed into Marco's face in blank astonishment.

Marco was the first to speak. "Oh, I say—I'm sorry," he stammered, "I didn't know you were—sick," he finished, confusedly.

The freckled little face opposite showed a quick dull red. Jimmy Nolan did not like to be reminded of his deformity; yet, in spite of his anger, his heart glowed at the remorseful sympathy in Marco's eyes.

"I'm not sick," he snapped, in a choky voice, "no more 'n you be! What you doin' on my corner, anyhow?"

"Your corner!"

"Sure—my corner! You're not one of the gang! I bet you two cents you aren't even a newsie. Where's your badge?"

"B-badge?" Marco was too dazed to say more.

Jimmy grinned derisively. "Well, if you aren't the fresh guy!" he jeered.

"Paper!" It was a sharp voice of command, and Jimmy heard it at once. Instantly he became the alert master of his trade. For the next ten minutes he paid no attention to Marco beyond making sure that he was not attempting to sell any more papers. Marco, however, was too dejected to do anything but stand disconsolately at one side, watching with wistful eyes this alluring whirl of business into which he might not enter. For he might not enter—of that Marco was very sure. Jimmy's words had carried conviction.

Marco's mind was quite made up when Jimmy, during a lull in trade, condescendingly strolled nearer and allowed himself to be accosted.

"Look a-here, you," began Marco, eagerly, "where can I get one of those badges, and how much do they cost? Oh, I won't take your corner, course," he hastened to add, as a quick challenge came into Jimmy's face.

Jimmy hesitated. A derisive answer was on the end of his tongue, when a sudden memory of a fight that was not fought to a finish sent a softer light to his eyes.

"Say, how old be you, kid?" he asked, not unkindly.

Marco almost said "ten," when a wisdom born of his experience in buying a "paper off the squire" in Gaylordville taught him caution.

"I'm fourteen," he said, promptly.

Jimmy was not the "squire," however, and Jimmy had the fearlessness of his convictions.

"Go on—ye aren't, neither," he scoffed. "I'm 'most fourteen myself. What you givin' us?"

"Fourteen—you!" There was unbelieving wonder in Marco's face.

Jimmy changed color and shifted his position uneasily. Again had his hated deformity come to the front, but this time he had only himself to blame.

"Well, I'm not—very tall, course," he stammered, "but I'm fourteen, 'most—and you aren't," he concluded, with unreasoning fierceness. "Cut it out!"

Marco was silent for a moment, before he asked a wary question: "How old do you have to be to sell 'em—papers, you know?"

"Why?"

"'Cause that's how old I am. I'm old enough to sell 'em. See?" And he met Jimmy's eyes unfalteringly.

Jimmy stared. Then he grinned his admiration.

"Gee, you aren't no freshie, after all. I reckon maybe I—"

"Paper! Here, boy!"

Jimmy heard the words and was off at once. From the doorway Marco watched him wistfully. He saw Jimmy dodge this way and that, and finally leap to the step of a moving car. He saw him slip, too, and lose his hold, and he saw the quick surging of the crowd toward the middle of the street. The next moment, with a frightened cry, he himself had dashed into the thickest of it.

CHAPTER 12

Those who saw the little hunchback newsboy fall from a car that Christmas Eve remembered that it was another boy, dark-haired and dark-eyed, who was almost the first to reach his side. He had dug his way to the center of the crowd by a vigorous use of sharp little fists and elbows, and he dropped to the ground at the boy's side with a low cry of sympathy.

"Say, be you hurt?"

The hunchback raised his head and pulled himself half upright. He saw the crowd, the car conductor, and the two policemen hurrying toward him. Then with a grip on Marco's arm that hurt, he answered loudly, so that all might hear:

"Naw! Forget it. Course I'm not hurt!" And he dragged himself to his feet. In Marco's ear he muttered: "Quick! Get me out of this before the cops get here—quick!"

So great was the urgency in Jimmy's voice that Marco lost no time. He was adept at forcing his way through crowds, and five minutes after the accident he was hurrying Jimmy into the seclusion of one of the quieter cross streets.

It was Jimmy who spoke first. "See here, you, kid—this isn't a walkin' match," he panted, clutching at Marco's arm.

Marco turned sharply.

"Say, you are hurt," he cried.

"Course I's hurt. It's my arm," moaned Jimmy. "My arm and—my back. Look a-here, I reckon I'll have to stop—a minute," he faltered, his face growing suddenly white. "My legs don't seem—to—go—

and the sidewalk does!"

Marco threw out a supporting arm and led the way to a doorstep. "But why didn't you tell them you were hurt?" he demanded.

In spite of his pain, Jimmy tossed him a scornful glance. "Tell 'em! Thanks! I don't want no hospital in mine."

Marco was silent. What a "hospital" might be, he did not know, but that it was bad he did not doubt, after Jimmy's words. Jimmy, too, was silent. He seemed to be debating something in his mind. At last he spoke, laboriously, painfully.

"See here, kid, what's your name?" he asked.

"Marco Ferdinando Bonelli."

"Gee! That all?" A flash of the old spirit looked out of Jimmy's eyes, but it faded as quickly as it had come. "Well, I reckon maybe, Marco What-d'-ye-call-it, you'll have to go home with me. Can ye?"

"Sure."

"Where you live?" asked Jimmy.

"Nowhere."

"Nowhere!" repeated Jimmy, in surprise.

"Well, I don't now. You see, I was with the organ-man; but I didn't like it there, and I got away. I'm lookin' for Flossie—but I've got plenty of time to take you home. How far is it?"

"Oh, it isn't far," muttered Jimmy, setting his teeth to hide the pain as he struggled to his feet. In spite of Jimmy's assertion, however, it did seem far to the little back room that Jimmy called home; and more than once Marco thought he would have to call for stronger arms than his to get his companion under shelter. But Jimmy did not quite lose strength until the top of the last flight of stairs was reached; then, with a jerk of his head toward the closed door in front of him, he fell in a little heap to the floor.

Marco knocked at the door and waited. He knocked again and still received no answer. Then he turned the knob softly and pushed open the door.

Across the room on a mattress in the corner lay a man asleep or drunk, Marco could not tell which. There were a table, a broken chair, two boxes, an old cradle holding a sleeping baby, and a rusty stove—fireless. By the light of a smoky kerosene lamp Marco could make out another mattress in the corner near the door; it was to this mattress that he decided he must try to get the hunchback. In the hall he stooped over the huddled little heap and touched it gently.

"Can't you walk—just a step? Or can't you just crawl?" he coaxed. "You hadn't ought to lie here on the floor."

There was no answer. Marco hesitated, then stooped and tried to lift the crooked little form. He had half dragged, half carried it inside the room when a thin, tired-looking woman carrying a bundle of kindling-wood and a small bag of coal, appeared in the doorway. With a startled cry she dropped her bundles and took the boy from Marco's arms.

"Jimmy! Jimmy, darlin'—what's ailin' ye?"

"He got hurt, ma'am. He fell off the car," explained Marco. "But he wasn't like this till just now. He could walk and talk."

"But he is hurt—he's hurt bad," moaned the woman, tenderly laying her burden on the old mattress in the corner. "Pat! Pat!" she called sharply, but the man in the other corner did not stir. With a look of disgust, the woman turned back to Marco. "See here, boy, you'll have to do! Run down to th' Settlement House and ask for Miss Dole. Tell her Jimmy Nolan is hurt; she'll have to come quick! It's the Settlement House, two blocks down on the corner. Anyone will tell you. Run, now!"

Marco did run. More than that, he found Miss Dole and brought her back with him, and then he had more errands to run, for her this time and also for the doctor. Long afterward, when both Miss

Dole and the doctor had gone, Mrs. Nolan suddenly awoke to a realization that he was still there, patiently awaiting orders.

"And you are still here?" she cried, contritely. "I didn't mean to be keeping you so late, so I didn't. Run home now, an'—thank you, kindly." Then something in the boy's face as he turned away made her ask: "Will it be far? Where your a-livin'?"

Marco shook his head. His eyes were on the rusty stove—fireless no longer. Outside it had begun to snow again, and he knew it. The stuffy, smoke-scented room, bare as it was, looked wonderfully inviting.

"It isn't far—and it isn't near," he answered at last. "It isn't—nowhere."

"Nowhere!"

From the corner where lay the hunchback in splints and bandages came a sudden stir. A voice, feeble but authoritative, spoke.

"Say, Ma, he's my friend, Marco What-d'ye-call-it, and he's going to stay with me tonight."

CHAPTER 13

Marco was awake early Christmas morning. From his position behind the stove (where he had curled himself to sleep like a cat the night before) he watched Pat Nolan bestir himself and get to his feet, angrily demanding something to eat. Not until the man had devoured his scanty, timidly-prepared breakfast and stumbled out of the room did Marco crawl from his hiding place and wish his hostess a cheery Merry Christmas.

To his distress, the woman burst into tears. "Sure, and it's no Christmas at all, at all," she moaned bitterly, "with Jimmy lyin' there like that, with his arm broke, and his poor crooked back all hurt."

"But he wasn't killed, and he's going to get better," comforted Marco. "The doctor said so."

"Yes, and who'll be after bringing in the money till he does, with the baby sick and me not workin'? Tell me that! And there's the doctor with his pills to pay for, an'—Oh, Jimmy, and be you awake, darlin'?" she broke off, hurrying across the room in answer to a feeble call.

Five minutes later she had left the room, a bit of money from Jimmy's pockets clutched in her hand. She was scarcely out of sight when the hunchback turned his feverish gaze on Marco.

"Look a-here, kid, what did he say—that doctor? When is I going to get out of this?" he catechized.

Marco shook his head. "He didn't say, but he said you weren't killed." Marco's voice was hopeful.

"Aw, did he now?" scoffed Jimmy, with an angry flounce that sent a quick spasm of pain across his face. "Well, anyhow, kid, I reckon

I'm up against it sure, this time," he moaned, turning away his head.

"Up against what?"

"Everything. Who's going to sell my papers? Who's going to get the dough for the grub?"

"But, your dad—"

"Dad!" It was a single word, but its intonation was unmistakable, and Marco said no more. Jimmy, however, did say more. "Dad? Why Dad's drunk when he isn't doin' time. It's 'cause of him I'm worrying. He licks Ma and me, too, when trade isn't good and there is nottin' comin' his way. I bet you two cents Ma didn't let on to him this mornin' I was hurt. I know her!"

Marco was silent. Then a sudden glow came to his face. "Jimmy, I'll sell your papers! Just tell me how to get 'em, and give me your badge," he cried excitedly, springing to his feet. "Quick, give it over! I'll be you!"

"Go on! What are you givin' us?" scouted Jimmy. "Just as if you could! Your eyes aren't blue, and your hair isn't red, aren't they?"

"Why, n-no."

"Well, mine are, and I signed a card that said they were. Do you think you look like me? Besides, the gang'd be on to you in no time. I tell you, there is no way out of it. I just got to get well, and—S-sh!" Mrs. Nolan had opened the door, and the baby had waked with a feeble cry.

Marco was very quiet during the next half hour. He accepted with thanks the frugal breakfast that Mrs. Nolan put before him; but at the first opportunity, when neither Jimmy nor his mother was looking at him, he picked up his cap and slipped out of the room.

Very swiftly, but with a careful noting of streets and turns, Marco sped back to the great station where he had left his violin the night before. He found the window without difficulty, and the man was still behind it, taking in bags and bundles. But to obtain the violin was not so easy.

To Marco it was all a curious jumble of checks that he ought to have and money that he could not pay. There were sharp words and many admonitions as to what he must and must not do in the future, and there were two or three men who had to be listened to patiently before the precious violin was finally thrust into his hands and he was free to hurry out upon the streets.

Never before had Marco played as he played that Christmas day. Behind every trill and run seemed to be Jimmy's wistful eyes urging him to do his best, and through every melody vibrated Jimmy's, "Who's going to get the dough for the grub?" Whatever was the message that the violin carried to the listener's ears, it was an effectual one; for seldom had the coins clinked so merrily in Marco's cap, and never before had Marco's smile been so joyous as he gathered them in.

All day he tramped the streets, pausing only for a hasty luncheon at noon. At night he counted his earnings, finishing with a joyous shout as he picked up his violin and dashed down the street toward Jimmy's home. Some minutes later Mrs. Nolan, softly crying in the stuffy little smoke-scented room, found herself confronted by a wild-eyed boy who poured a jingling wealth of coins into her lap.

"I did it!" he cried. "I did it all today. And I'm going to do it tomorrow, and tomorrow, and tomorrow, until Jimmy gets well. And you needn't be licked, and Jimmy needn't, neither, 'cause I'm going to earn the grub!"

CHAPTER 14

Marco had been with the Nolans four months. He was in school now, a part of the time—Miss Dole had seen to that. He was a newsboy, too, and Miss Dole had helped him to that. He had a badge all his own, and he, like Jimmy, had signed a card whereon was stated the color of his hair and eyes, his name, his weight, his height, and various other items of information, all of which were quite unnecessary, in Marco's opinion. He was a member of the "gang," too. Jimmy—long since recovered from his injury—had seen to that. And on the whole, in Marco's estimation of himself, he was eminently prosperous. Only one cloud showed above his horizon—but that cloud was growing larger every day: Flossie was not yet found.

Money matters at the Nolans were very simple. While Jimmy, the chief breadwinner, was incapacitated, Marco turned over all that he earned to Mrs. Nolan. After Jimmy's recovery, Marco kept half for himself. Pat Nolan for some days after Marco's arrival had been a terror and a troublesome expense; but he disappeared after a time, and Jimmy came home one day with the cheery announcement that his father was "jugged" and would not be out for six months. After that the little family in the back room up three flights breathed more easily, and ceased to shudder at every shuffling step on the stairs.

April passed and May came. In the little oases of green in the city squares where two streets crossed, spring awoke and touched everything with her magic hand. There was the smell of green things growing and the sound of birds twittering in the tree branches. Along the windowed walls of the tenements, the spindling geraniums lifted their heads and blossomed into flecks of red and pink and white; and even in the refuse-strewn backyards, patches of courageous green appeared. Out on the sidewalk, the children swarmed with their hoops and balls and roller skates, and on the steps and curbstones the women tended their babies and called to each other merrily. Unmistakably spring had come.

It was then that Mrs. Nolan noticed a changed in Marco. The boy had grown even thinner and paler, and his eyes looked out wistfully from cavernous depths. His steps lagged, and he ate almost nothing. His earnings, too, grew scantier day by day, though there was every evidence that he tried valiantly to keep up with Jimmy and the other boys in his paper selling. He seldom touched the violin now, and he often perched himself in the window, only to sit there motionless, with his eyes on the broken line of roofs outside.

Twice Mrs. Nolan questioned him, but she got no answer that was satisfactory. He was well, and there was not anything the matter, he said.

June came, but matters grew only worse. Marco was almost ill now. He still sold papers—or tried to sell them—but his thin little voice could not rise above the roar of the streets, and his stumbling feet failed half the time to reach the prospective customer before it was too late. Even Jimmy eyed him curiously and jeered a little at his ill-success. At last he questioned him peremptorily, but not unkindly.

"Look a-here, kid, what's up?" he demanded. "Ye've been off your feed for a month. There isn't a freshie on the street who can beat you out in no time—walkin' backwards, too! What's up?"

"Nothin'."

"Cut it out! Dar is too, and you knows it."

Marco shook his head and stumbled off to catch a passing car, and Jimmy had no choice but to turn to his own affairs. An hour later, however, business was over for the day, and then Jimmy probed the boy again. This time he was more successful; he found out what was the matter.

Until noon the next day—which happened to be Sunday—he

pondered over what Marco had said to him; then he sought Miss Dole at the Settlement House.

"Well, Jimmy," she smiled, "what can I do for you?"

Jimmy choked and cleared his throat. "Well, you see, ma'am," he stammered, "I came to see if you'd let me off from going to that 'ere place this summer where I went the last two years."

"Let you off! Why, Jimmy, you can't mean Mont-Lawn!"

"Yes'm, that's it, Mont-Lawn."

"But, Jimmy, I thought you liked to—to go there," remonstrated Miss Dole, plainly puzzled.

Jimmy's chin quivered, but his head came up with a defiant jerk. "Sure, but I been there twice, and Marco, he hasn't never. I thought maybe you'd let him go—in my place." In spite of the air of defiant nonchalance, Miss Dole caught the break in Jimmy's voice and understood.

"Yes, I see," she said gently, after a moment. "You want Marco to go in your place."

"Well, Marco, he's sick," explained Jimmy, gaining new courage, now that the plunge had been taken. "And last night he let on a lot how he's feelin'. He isn't used to cities like I am, and he run on somethin' awful about wantin' to be out in the country where there's room to get your breath. Oh, he wants it. He wants it somethin' awful; and I remembered that Mont-Lawn's like that, and I don't need it, course, bein' well and strong, so I thought maybe you'd let him go in my place. Say, will ye?"

For a moment Miss Dole did not answer. She was looking at the little twisted form before her that was so "well and strong," and she was thinking of the stories that had come to her of how this same little lad had reveled in the fun and sunshine and good food of the Children's Vacation Home during the two visits he had made there.

"Very well, Jimmy," she said at last, slowly, "I'll see what I can do. Perhaps I'll look up Marco myself some day."

"Thank you," mumbled Jimmy, rising precipitately to his feet and stumbling out of the room. It had come to him just then with an overwhelming force what a dreary thing life was going to be, after all, with no ten-days' visit to Mont-Lawn to look forward to—the object of his dreams all winter.

Yet to Marco, an hour later, he said, "I reckon maybe I've got some of that 'ere country doin's for you, kid. There's a place up the river where folks pays three dollars to take kids like you, and give them ten days out of doors. And there's girls there, too. Maybe that yaller-haired sister of your'n what's lost'll be one of 'em; who knows?"

CHAPTER 15

Perhaps among all the seventy children that met at the Bible House that June afternoon at one o'clock, there was none quite so happy as the dark-eyed, white-faced boy with the violin-case clutched tightly in his hand. Beside him, it is true, there was another little lad, a hunchback, whose face was scarcely less eager. Just how Miss Dole had managed to procure permission for both to go to Mont-Lawn, Jimmy did not know, but he and Marco agreed that somewhere in the world there must be some very kind people indeed who had made it possible.

To Jimmy this medical examination in the little room at the top of the Bible House was an old story, but to Marco it was all very new and interesting. It was a little fearsome, too; for behind the screen in the corner was a doctor, before whom each child must pass. Twice Marco had seen a boy come away with red eyes and quivering chin—something was the matter, and he could not go. What if he, too, could not go? What if he, too, must go back to the hated bricks and alley-ways? Where, then, would be his ten beautiful days of grass and trees and room to breathe? Marco grew faint with the horror of the fear that he could not go—then his name was called, and he found himself dizzily crossing the room to that fateful screen in the corner.

He smiled, afterward, to think how soon it was all over. A quick, but a very keen glance at his eye, his ear, and his throat, with something thrust for a moment into his mouth; then a gentle turn toward the other room, which meant that he might go; and that was all. Jimmy, too, came almost at once, and together they joined the chattering, laughing swarms of boys and girls waiting for the order to start.

Marco took time then to look about him. He was thinking of Flossie. There were girls, plenty of them: big, little, tall, short, blue-eyed, black-eyed, light-haired, and dark-haired; but nowhere was the one he sought, and he said as much to Jimmy.

"Pooh! Just hold your hosses," retorted Jimmy, airily. "This isn't the only pebbles on the beach—there's heaps more already up here. You just wait and see!"

The ride to Tarrytown in the special car, the trip across the Hudson to Nyack, and the scramble for places in the big four-seated carriages that were waiting to take them to Mont-Lawn—it was all very wonderful to Marco. Already now he could see trees and grass and far-reaching blue sky. Already his dream was coming true.

He was on the front seat of the first carriage with the driver. For long minutes they had been climbing up, up, up. On each side of them were the cool, green woods, and above their heads were the birds, singing. On the seat behind a boy crowed, "Just look at the black-eyed Susies!" And the cry was taken up with a shout, and echoed from half a dozen lusty throats.

To Marco it was almost too good to be true—and he was to have ten whole days of it! He was quite hugging himself with joy when suddenly the carriage swept around the last curve, and he saw the strangest sight he had ever seen in his life: two hundred children lined up along the fence shouting in a chorus of high treble. Just what they were shouting Marco could not make out until he had almost reached the lodge gates; then he caught the words:

"Spring chicken today! Spring chicken today!"

There was no time to answer. The carriage rolled through the gates and up the driveway. Marco's dazed eyes swept the sloping green lawns, the pretty cottages, the fields, and the woods beyond, and rested finally on the shimmering silver of the Hudson far to the east, where the sky came down to meet the earth.

To the homesick little lad so long hungering for the blessed out-of-doors, it was overwhelming. With a quick-drawn, sobbing breath, he began to cry.

The carriage stopped before the door of the Homestead, and a sweet-faced woman with anxious eyes hurried down the steps.

"Why, my dear! My dear child, what is it?" she called. "Are you hurt? Or ill?"

Marco shook his head. He was ashamed and distressed, but the tears still flowed.

"But what is it? What is the matter?" she urged.

"It—it's nothing" sobbed Marco. "It's only the g-grass, and the—sk-ky; and it seems as if it just couldn't be true!"

The woman looked away suddenly, with moist eyes. Then she turned to Marco and held out her hand. "But it is true," she said, brightly. "Just get down and see if it isn't. Oh, and you've brought your violin, too! Can you play?"

"You bet he can, Miss Denny," cried Jimmy, who had already jumped to the ground. "I'm Jimmy, don't you remember? And this is Marco, me friend. He's just dyin' for a place big enough to breathe in, and I told him you had it up here to beat the band. And you has, isn't you, Miss Denny?"

"We certainly have, Jimmy," laughed Miss Denny, a little

unsteadily. "And we hope you'll both be very, very happy. And here is Miss Bird looking for you. You're to be her boys this time, and she'll tell you where to put your things."

Marco turned and found a pair of merry brown eyes smiling down at him. They belonged to a pretty young woman in a white dress who already had gathered around her a dozen other boys about Marco's size.

"Come," she said, "and I'll show you your locker, and where you are to sleep. Then Jimmy shall show you the rest of Mont-Lawn."

CHAPTER 16

Wonders for Marco began at once. First, there were the beautiful grounds themselves, to say nothing of the swings, the see-saws, the sand pile, and the swimming-pool. Then at supper time came the signal from the great bell on the Homestead veranda. Marco was a little awkward about falling into line. He did not know just what was expected of him; but Jimmy and the teachers helped, and at last he stood, cap in hand, with the other boys forming a long double line extending far down the driveway in front of the Homestead. At still another stroke of the bell the lines separated, leaving a space between, through which the girls were to march to the great pavilion, where supper was waiting. Marco was excited indeed now, for Jimmy had whispered in his ear:

"Now's your time to watch. It's the girls; and maybe one of 'em'll be the one you're a-huntin' for."

Flossie!

Marco's heart leaped at the thought. Away at the rear where the girls, too, were in line, he could catch tantalizing glimpses of short gingham skirts and flaxen pigtails; and those skirts and pigtails were to come marching two by two past the spot where he stood. What if—

The teacher in the lead had started, and Marco held his breath. Now was the time!

Right, left, right, left. Two, four, six, eight, ten had passed. Right, left, right, left. Marco's eyes were wide and anxious. Right, left, right, left. On and on they came, chuckling, laughing, merry-faced. Right, left, right, left. The boys were falling in now. The girls had passed—and Flossie was not there.

It was a bitter disappointment to Marco, but Jimmy, as usual, had his words of comfort.

"Forget it. There's odders comin'. They bring new kids up here two, three times a week, and she'll be one of 'em, sure!"

The long tables, too, in the big pavilion had their comfort to offer Marco; for surely it was not in the nature of a hungry small boy to be quite downhearted in the face of all the good things to eat that those delightful tables held.

Later, in the beautiful Children's Temple, came the song service, with a word of praise and prayer; to Marco this was the most wonderful experience yet. The songs, the quiet hush, and the purple and gold and ruby light falling through the great stained-glass windows filled him with awed rapture. He knew the name God. He had heard it on the streets every day. But here it was different. It was not spoken in anger or with jeering laughter, but with gentleness and reverence. He remembered now that long ago, before his mother had been so ill, she had told him of this Being; and she, too, had spoken this way. It appeared that He was really good and kind and that He loved boys and girls and cared whether they were bad or not. Marco remembered now that his mother had said that too, but he had forgotten it of late.

The short vesper service was soon over, and Marco and his companions were out for another half hour of play before the great bell summoned them all to the little white beds in the cottages.

The sun was shining brightly when Marco awoke the next morning. He rubbed his eyes and opened them suddenly. Then he sat up and looked about him. No, it had not been a dream. Through the window he could see the blue sky and the green trees. And with a whoop of glee, he caught up his pillow and aimed straight for

Jimmy's small round head six feet away.

Mont-Lawn and all its people had a great surprise that morning. Marco took out his violin and began to play soon after breakfast, and it was not five minutes before he had an admiring group about him that grew moment by moment larger and more enthusiastic. Even the teachers stopped to listen and to marvel at the runs and trills and tripping melodies; a score of boys and girls were dancing before he had played half as many minutes. He had stopped, and they were begging for more, when at last he raised his violin and began to play "Lost on the Ocean Wave."

It was then that there came from one of the cottages a small girl on the run.

"See here, you—boy," she panted. "Is your name 'Marco'? There's a girl in there what says she knows you. She says she knows that tune you're a-playin'. She wants you to come. She hurt her foot yesterday mornin', and she can't come out here. Teacher says you're to go in there and see her."

Marco almost dropped his violin for joy. At last it had come—this thing he had dreamed of—Flossie had heard and had known him. He had found Flossie! With a glad little cry, he sprang forward, and ran for the steps of the cottage. His limbs shook, and his head swam dizzily; but he plunged blindly on and into the small room by the door where the teacher stood waiting for him.

"I've found you—oh, I've found you!" he called, rapturously.

"Marco! Gee, it is you!" cried a joyful voice.

Marco stopped short. All the light and joy fled from his face and left it blank with dismay. Before him was a dark-eyed, dark-haired, dark-skinned little maid who was clapping her hands in gleeful welcome.

"Annetta!" he choked. "And I thought—you—was—Flossie!"

Annetta sobered instantly.

"Gee, you didn't, now! Say, that was tough luck! But aren't you a little mite glad to see me?"

"Why, yes, of course, I'm awful glad," returned Marco dully. "But I thought you were—Flossie."

It took all the tact and skill of the teacher and all the merriest wiles of Annetta to bring back the smiles to Marco's face, and even then the boy did not quite forget that woeful moment when he saw the dusky curls of Annetta where he had thought to find the golden locks of the long-lost Flossie.

CHAPTER 17

One by one the days passed. Long as they were from dawn until dark, they were not long enough for the wonderful walks and games and frolics that filled them to the brim.

Marco's face was not now so white and wan, and his cheeks were not so hollow. His eyes, too, no longer looked out wistfully from cavernous depths. In spite of his disappointment at not finding Flossie, he was very happy, and the place rang merrily all day long with the cheery tones of his violin.

The teachers wondered sometimes what they would do when Marco went away. His playing was so delightful both to themselves and to the children. There was no one, indeed, at Mont-Lawn who did not at one time or another fall captive to the charm of Marco's music, from the chef in the kitchen to the Italian laborers who kept the paths and driveways so beautifully clean.

Four days before Marco was to go home came the Fourth, and a "glorious Fourth" it was indeed for Marco, from the pop of the first firecracker in the morning to the swish of the last rocket at night.

At noon guests had come from far and near, until the audience on the lawn was a thousand strong; both there and at the exercises in the Temple hundreds of sturdy throats rent the air with cheers.

Marco knew the songs now and could sing with a will. He knew the "Allegiance to the Flag," too, and with the best of them he could place his hand on his heart, and look toward the flag above the platform, and chant the salutation. It always stirred him—the sight of that flag and the sound of those hundreds of ringing voices chanting in unison—but never before had it swept over him with quite the force that it carried today. Perhaps it was because that on the platform was a great man, a hero of a score of battles, who had come to speak to them; and perhaps it was because of what he had just said about the flag.

"It is not the flag of a king or an emperor or a president. It is the flag of the people. It is your flag, and its very colors mean something. Red stands for valor—and the blood that's been shed. Blue stands for justice—it's the true blue of our hearts. And white stands for purity and loyalty—the purity and loyalty of a brave boy's soul when he does what he knows is right!"

All this the great man had said, and much more. And to it all, Marco had listened intently. It had stirred him strangely. Marco had known little about bravery and justice and loyalty. They had been dead words to him; but now they suddenly became alive with warmth and meaning, and they burned their message deep into his soul. The whole day became a glorious red, white, and blue. The whole day became a flag. The red of the firecrackers, the blue of the sky, and the white of the holiday dresses were to his imaginative mind but so many flags waving a joyous salute to their country. Even as he fell asleep that night, Marco was still humming the last strains of "The Red, White, and Blue."

It was the next morning that Marco first noticed the man who stopped to listen to his playing. He was one of the Italian laborers who kept the paths in order, and Marco noticed that after that first time the man loitered very often near the music, and that he looked at him with peculiar intentness. The next day Marco was walking alone along the path when he saw the man again. This time the man stopped his work and spoke to him.

"You play well, boy. Who taught you?" The words came distinctly, with no trace of an accent, which vaguely surprised Marco. From the man's looks, he would have expected something quite different.

"My mother."

The man lifted his head with a peculiar gesture and came nearer. "Boy, what is your name?" he asked.

Marco hesitated. Instinctively he backed nearer to the iron railing. There was something about this questioning that he did not like.

"Marco," he answered, shortly.

"I thought so," muttered the man. "Marco Ferdinando Bonelli, eh?"

Marco stared blankly. "Why, how did you—oh, somebody must have told you, of course," he finished, with some doubt.

"Yes, somebody told me," nodded the man, slowly. Then he stopped talking and went to raking vigorously—Miss Denny was coming along the path.

Marco seemed always to be running across the man after that, and every time the man stopped and said something. He was very pleasant and seemed to be trying to make friends with him. He knew a great deal about many curious things, too, that were wonderfully interesting to a small boy, and Marco came to like him and to watch for him. On the day before his visit was to close, Marco himself accosted the man to say goodbye.

"You see, I'm going away tomorrow," he explained, sorrowfully. "My time is up."

The man hesitated. He looked swiftly about him. They were at the end of the path, and there was no one else near. For a moment he looked at Marco in silence, then he spoke, his face flushing a dull red.

"Marco, did your mother ever speak of—your—dad?"

"Once—or twice."

"What did she say?"

"Nothin' much."

"But what was it?"

Marco drew his brows together in a frown before he answered, slowly, "It wasn't so much what she said as how she looked."

"Oh!" The man pulled at the collar of his coarse shirt as if it hurt him. After a time, he spoke again. "Didn't you ever wonder where he was?"

"Why, maybe. I dun know."

"Wouldn't you—like it if you could—see him?"

Marco considered.

"I don't think—I would," he said, with some deliberation. "I don't think he was good to Mumsey."

"But he meant to be. He always meant to be. It was only that he—" The man stopped abruptly, refusing to meet the boy's widening eyes.

"But how do you know that?" demanded Marco. "How do you know he—" The boy stopped, a growing terror in his eyes. Suddenly he realized that this man had known his name, "Marco Ferdinando Bonelli," that he had known many other little things about him before he was told, that he looked strangely like the picture in his mother's locket, and that he was standing now shame-faced and trembling, as if—

"You can't be—Dad!" stammered the boy.

"And if I was?" The man turned sharply with the question.

He had his answer in the way the boy fell back before his approach.

"But you mustn't—you don't know! I am your dad!" cried the man, feverishly. "And I'm hungry for you. You're my boy. I need you. I want you. I'll take care of you, too. You must come!" And he poured into Marco's ears an appeal that stirred the boy as had the words of the great man about the flag on the Fourth of July. To Marco they seemed alike, too—those appeals. He must be brave, be true, be loyal; he must do what was right. But what was right? It was all so confusing. He must think it out alone. He could not decide now.

"I'll tell you in the mornin', 'fore I go," he promised, falteringly; then he hurried away.

They sang "The Red, White, and Blue" in the song service that night, and someone gave them a little talk on what it meant to be brave, loyal sons of God, of their country, and of their fathers and mothers on earth. Before Marco went to sleep that night, his decision was made.

The man looked haggard and as if he had not slept when Marco saw him just before it was time to start for the ferry. But his face lighted up so wonderfully when Marco told him his decision that the boy felt a curiously choking lump rise in his throat.

"Come to the Grand Central tonight at six o'clock," said the man, huskily. "I'll be there to meet you, and after that you'll be my boy—mine."

Marco went back to New York with Jimmy and the others a little sadly. Behind him lay the trees and the grass and the ten days of delight. Before him lay the city and a new life with a man who was a stranger. But in his ears were ringing the strains of "The Red, White, and Blue," and in his heart was a stern determination. He would do right. He would be loyal, brave, and true.

At Mont-Lawn that night the boss of the laborers reported to Miss Denny a man missing. He had slipped away some time during the day and had been seen apparently going to New York. His place would be filled at once, however, the boss said, and the work would not suffer.

CHAPTER 18

Marco told only Jimmy where he was going.

"It's Dad—I've found him," he explained tersely, silencing Jimmy's expostulations afterward with a short, "But bein' Dad—so, I've got to go, don't you see?"

In the great station Marco found the man waiting for him at six o'clock, and together they went out upon the street.

"I don't have much of a place yet to take you to," apologized the man nervously, "but it'll be better soon. I've got you now—somethin' worth workin' for."

Marco had been wondering all day what his father's home would be like. Since giving his promise that morning he had grown fearful. With a shudder he remembered his experience with the organ-grinder—he certainly did not want to repeat that. In spite of himself, since living with Jimmy, he had come to share that youth's aversion to "Dagoes," and for some time he had made little use of his surname.

As he trudged along now by the man's side, he needed all his courage to keep himself from slipping away at the nearest corner; and he had to repeat over and over to himself all that he could remember of what the great man on the Fourth of July had said about truth, and loyalty, and duty bravely performed. So busy was he, indeed, lashing himself into the proper frame of mind, that he was surprised when his companion stopped before a door leading to a basement tenement. He was more surprised when a quick glance about him told him that the place was not two blocks away from where he had been living for six months with the Nolans.

Inside the house the man led the way through a dark hallway and evil-smelling kitchen to a small bedroom lighted by a narrow window on a level with the sidewalk.

"You see, it isn't much," he said, wistfully.

"But is it ours?—all ours?—this room?" demanded Marco.

"Yes—when I pay. Milanovitch—I get it off him. He lives there,"—with a jerk of his thumb toward the evil-smelling kitchen. "He has two rooms, but he's got a wife and five kids. I've got a kid now. I've got you!" And he looked at Marco with a curious longing in his eyes.

Marco shifted his position and gazed about the room. He was embarrassed and ill at ease. He wished he were back with Jimmy Nolan. He feared he was not going to like this new father, who acted so strangely, and who looked at one so curiously. He realized, too, uncomfortably, that something was expected of himself, but it was a full minute before he managed to stammer:

"It's very nice, I'm sure—this room."

There was a moment's silence. The man, now, was embarrassed. At last he spoke, but with evident effort.

"You haven't said 'Dad' once, yet. Did you know it?"

The boy flushed; then he blurted out the one question that had been close to his lips all the evening—and it was the one question that he had meant not to ask.

"Dad, am I—a Dago?"

The man scowled angrily. For a moment he looked as if he would strike the boy; then his hand fell impotently.

"We better eat," he said, in a dull voice, turning to some packages he had brought with him. "Maybe then we'll talk."

It was a frugal meal and soon over. Marco was not hungry and did not eat much. The man, too, ate little and was silent. Out in the kitchen, a babel of angry jargon told that Milanovitch had come home—and with a bad temper. Everywhere strange sights and sounds met Marco's eyes and ears. Nothing was familiar save the smoky odor of the kerosene lamp, and that brought only homesick memories of the Nolans.

Not for some time after he had finished eating did the man speak; then he began slowly: "You might as well know now right away that your name isn't Bonelli," he said. "It's Covino."

"Covino!"

"Yes."

"But, what for? How is it? Who said—"

The man stopped the torrent of questions with an imperative gesture.

"It's too late to go into all that—and it wouldn't do no good if I did. What's necessary, I'll tell you. I'm John Covino, and you're my boy, so your name's Covino."

"And was you—a gypsy?"

"Maybe—and maybe not. I was with them—when you were born."

"But you went away; you must have went away. Mumsey told me she didn't know where you were."

To Marco's surprise the man turned away his head suddenly. The next moment his face was in his hands, and he was sobbing bitterly. Marco watched him with growing uneasiness. In his own throat that curious lump was coming again. He was distressed, embarrassed, and angry with the man; yet within himself a strange, imperative something was even at that moment dragging him to his feet. In obedience he crossed the room and touched the man on his shoulder.

"Dad, I—" He could not say more. The man had him in an embrace that hurt.

CHAPTER 19

One by one the weeks passed; Marco found that his daily life was not so much changed, after all. He still sold papers and still belonged to the "gang." He saw Jimmy frequently, and sometimes he visited the Nolan home. He lived, to be sure, in the little room out of the Milanovitch kitchen; and he was the object of the most slavish devotion on the part of a man who worked all day at one of the wharves only to invest his earnings in something for the pleasure or the comfort of "my boy, Marco."

Neighbors who had known John Covino during the past year could scarcely believe the evidence of their own senses now. They had known before that he could work, and work well—when there was no liquor to be had. But they had known, too, that his employers must keep a sharp lookout and see that temptation was never put in his way. They were amazed now to see the man start day after day for his work, with erect shoulders and a steady eye; and they were more amazed to see him return each Saturday night with money in his pocket and no liquor in his stomach. They told each other that it was a good thing that Covino had found his boy. They had always liked him, they said. He was a good fellow—when he was not drunk.

In September Marco went into school again. He was still looking for Flossie—and still in vain. Twice he had questioned John Covino concerning her, but he had learned nothing; the man did not seem to wish to talk of her.

"It wasn't Dad, then, that come after her," Marco had muttered to himself afterward, "'cause if it was, he'd a-known now where she was. It must ha' been some other man."

Marco had been in school two weeks when, one Saturday night, John Covino did not come home at supper time. Seven, eight, nine o'clock came, and still he did not appear. Marco was puzzled and almost frightened. Not once since they had lived together had the man failed to be there at the appointed time, gleefully displaying some dainty he had bought for their supper.

Ten o'clock came, and with it an unsteady step outside the door. At the sound Marco sprang to his feet. A vision of Pat Nolan dimmed his eyes; then the door burst open.

"Dad!"

The man braced himself against the door, balancing on unsteady legs before reeling across the room to the nearest chair. Marco sprang to the door and closed it; then he turned and faced his father.

"Dad!"

The man lifted his chin, half aggressively, half jauntily. "Well, what do you have to say?" he demanded, thickly.

"Dad, Oh, Dad! How could you?"

The man's gaze drifted from the boy's shocked face and roved unsteadily about the tiny room, resting finally on the violin which Marco had been playing.

"Give us—a tune, boy," he muttered. "I like—tunes."

Mechanically Marco picked up the violin and began to play. He was trying to think what to say, what to do, but he was stunned and confused. To his relief the bleared eyes opposite closed after a time, and the huddled form in the chair relaxed in sleep; then Marco laid down his violin and hurried out into the kitchen.

"Look a-here, was Dad ever—like this—before?" he begged,

tremulously, of Milanovitch, who was dozing by the stove.

Milanovitch's broken English was not easy to understand, but in time Marco had his answer.

Yes, John Covino had been like this before, but not for some time. He had fallen in tonight with some old companions and had evidently yielded to their entreaties to take a drink. Milanovitch himself had seen him only an hour before, down at the saloon on the corner, and he had been drinking then heavily. Milanovitch was sorry, but there was nothing that he could do—nothing. And Marco could only turn and go sorrowfully back to the little room that was worse than empty.

It was pitiful to see John Covino's shame and remorse when he awoke to a realization of what he had done. He blamed himself bitterly and made many protestations of future good conduct—yet October was not two weeks old when, again, Marco came home Saturday night to find a silent, unlighted room.

Milanovitch brought word this time that Covino was "fighting drunk" down at the saloon. He was certainly scarcely less than that when he finally came home at eleven o'clock.

For half an hour, Marco dodged blows and winced at angry curses. For half an hour, he exerted all his skill to pacify the rum-crazed brain; then he remembered his violin and began to play.

The bleared eyes did not close in slumber this time, but they did lose their angry fire. Gradually the twitching muscles and menacing fists fell quiet. The oaths and snarls of rage ceased. The man sat silent, listening. Afterward he yielded to Marco's entreaties and was put to bed like a child.

It is hard to say whether John Covino was the more angry or the more ashamed when his befogged reason finally cleared. Certainly he could not endure Marco's sorrowful eyes, and at the first opportunity he fled from their mute reproach. From himself he could not flee—though he tried to; he made straight for the saloon on the corner that he might drown memory in drink. That night he did not return at all, and Marco lay in his bed and shivered at every sound outside the door.

It was the beginning of the end. More and more frequently as the days passed, Marco came home to find an empty room and no supper. Entreaties and pleadings were in vain. There were promises—plenty of them and even tears; but the promises were scarcely made before they were broken, and the tears only served to emphasize the weakness of a man who wept because he drank—and then drank because he wept. Even the violin failed sometimes to bring peace, though it was the most potent weapon that Marco possessed. So potent, indeed, was it, that one night Milanovitch suggested that Marco take it down to the saloon and see if he could not lure Covino home.

In the saloon Marco faced a crowd of amazed, jeering men. He would have backed out in dismay had not John Covino at that moment caught sight of him.

"It's my boy! It's Marco!" he exulted, staggering across the room. "He's going to play—he is. He plays good—good!" And with an unsteady hand laid on the boy's shoulder, he turned and tried to make a bow to the staring men.

Marco flushed and tugged at his father's coat.

"Dad, Dad, come home!" he implored. "Come home now, and I will play to ye—truly I will. Come!"

Covino frowned. His clasp on the boy's shoulder tightened.

"Home? No! It's better here. All light—all warm. Play!" he commanded.

Marco drew back.

"No, no, Dad—come home! I'll play there."

With an angry snarl the man jerked the boy to the right-about and held him there while he delivered himself of a tirade, the burden of which was that the boy was his and that he was going to play, that he could play and he should play, that things were at a pretty pass, indeed, when a mere slip of a lad could defy his father like that and refuse to entertain his father's friends.

Marco raised his violin then and began to play. He could see no other way out of it. He hoped that the music would have an effect—and it did, but not the one he expected. He had looked to see his father become docilely willing to accompany him home; he found, instead, a score of men decidedly unwilling that even he himself should go home. With a drunken cheer they demanded more and yet more, and with an oath one cried:

"Set them up on me for the fiddlin' kid!"

John Covino found out then how he could get more drinks, even though he had no more money. Again and again he ordered the boy to play, and again and again some man among the crowd was moved to treat. Marco himself was powerless in their hands, and in sheer terror was forced to submit. Only when the "cop" looked in did he have a respite from playing, and then only while he was being hidden behind the men until the officer left the saloon. Not until nearly midnight was Marco finally allowed to lead home the man who was almost too stupefied to put one foot before the other.

Sorry days dawned then for Marco. Covino lost his job at the wharves and obtained another and another only to lose them both through drink. When sober he was all tears, all repentance, all eager promises to Marco to do better. When drunk—when drunk he forced the boy to play and earn either the drinks themselves or the money that would buy them.

Marco was in despair. There was little money coming in now, and food was scanty. The pawnshop was daily growing richer by John Covino's frequent visits, and the little room off Milanovitch's kitchen was growing correspondingly bare.

Jimmy Nolan, who for some time watched the struggle in silence, was finally goaded into wrathful remonstrance.

"Why don't you quit, and come back to us, Marco?" he protested at last. "We'll take you in, and be glad to."

Marco made a gesture of dissent.

"No," he said, decidedly. "I just can't. You see, it's this way," he explained with some hesitation. "Dad's mine, and I ought to stick to him; there is not much that is mine. Every feller ought to have somethin' to be red, white, and blue too, like a flag, you know. Now, I'm shady on flags, bein' as how I'm not really sure whether I—I'm a Da—well, I'm not real sure what I am. But I have got a dad, and I've just got to be red, white, and blue to him!"

CHAPTER 20

In the great hall of one of the stone palaces facing Central Park, Howard Preston hung up the receiver and turned slowly away from the telephone. On his face was a peculiar expression, half eager, half regretful. Even his mother, coming down the stairs, noticed it.

"Well, Howard," she smiled, "from your face I don't know whether to congratulate you or to commiserate you. Which shall it be?"

"That's exactly it," laughed the young fellow. "I don't know myself."

"What is it?"

"Well, I—" He hesitated and placed a caressing arm around the waist of the woman as together they entered the library. "Well, Mother dear, I—I have just had a communication that my—brother needs me."

"Your—brother!" The mother of an only son drew back in amazement.

The man laughed.

"Oh, the relationship is very recent and very sudden," he retorted, whimsically, "and I fancy he won't, by even the greatest stretch of his imagination, attempt to include you in his family."

"Howard, what are you talking about? What is the meaning of all this nonsense?"

One of the curious changes, that were perhaps Howard Preston's greatest charm, crossed the young man's face and left it alight with purpose.

"Forgive me, Mater, for my justing. It isn't nonsense at all, as you'll see. I told you the other night, didn't I, about Dr. Fernald's lecture on the Children's Court?"

"Yes."

"Well, it's that. You know at the time we asked him what we could do, and he told us. We agreed, and it's come. That's all."

"What's come?"

"My 'brother.' I agreed, you know, to hold myself in readiness for the work."

"But Dr. Fernald is so unrealistic, Howard. As if you had any business with courts and policemen and—and jails!"

"That's exactly it, Mater! I haven't any business with courts and policemen and jails; it's only with the boy that the court turns over to me. And Dr. Fernald isn't unrealistic a bit. He's as practical as—as a fire when it's cold. If you'd only heard him, Mother, when he said in that ringing, live voice of his, 'Men, I want each one of you to take just one boy who has been in trouble. I want you to help him at this critical moment. I want you to be a big brother to him.'"

"A brother!"

"A big brother," nodded the man, the old whimsical smile coming back to his face. "I'm half an inch and six feet tall. I weigh one hundred and seventy pounds, and I'm twenty-one years and three weeks old. Surely, may I not be a big brother?"

Mrs. Preston opened her lips, but before she could speak, a

childish treble from across the room broke the silence.

"You aren't anyone's big brother but mine," it called decisively.

In spite of her disquietude, Mrs. Preston laughed. "You see," she said, with a wave of her hands, "you are answered."

Across the room a pair of blue-violet eyes, topped with a white forehead and a fluff of yellow hair, looked out from between the tightly held curtains of the window alcove. Then the curtains dropped suddenly, and a twelve-year-old girl, all in white, from slippers to hair ribbon, stood revealed.

"Well, Puss, and what are you doing?" demanded the prospective big brother.

"I was reading, when you came in—and interrupted."

"Books, books, always books, Kittykins! And was it a prince or a princess that was imprisoned this time?"

The small girl advanced, her chin up-tilted, and seated herself on an upholstered footstool a few feet away.

"It wasn't either," she retorted with dignity. "It was a young lady. I shall be a young lady in four months. I shall be thirteen then. This young lady's name was 'Helen Annabel Augusta Miranda.'"

"Dear me! All that? Only fancy, Fluff, if you had that!"

"Me!" cried the little girl, aggrievedly. "Me! And if I did, I suppose I'd be twenty-'leven hundred more names. Even now I'm 'Fluff,' and 'Fluffy-top,' and 'Puss,' and 'Kittykins,' and 'Flossie,' and 'Floy,' and—"

"And a dear, whatever you are—Florence," interrupted the young man with mock gravity.

"And I'm 'Mater' and 'Mother' and 'Sweetheart,' and those are only a few of my names," reminded Mrs. Preston, laughingly.

"And I'm a big brother," said the man, with a gravity that was not mocking.

"Yes, you're my big brother," affirmed Florence.

"Oh, but I'm somebody else's big brother, too, now."

"Whose?"

"I'm not real sure yet that I know his name. But I think it's Covino, or something like that."

"Covino! Howard, how can you do it?" murmured Mrs. Preston, shuddering.

"That's exactly what I mean to find out," smiled the man. "I expect Dr. Fernald's going to tell me how I can do it."

Mrs. Preston sighed and shook her head, but the child crept nearer.

"And are you his big brother?"

"I said I'd be."

"Then am I his sister?"

"No, no, child!" cried Mrs. Preston, in quick horror. Even the man frowned.

"Well, that hardly—follows," he said, grimly.

"But will you bring him home—here?" persisted the little girl.

Mrs. Preston rose to her feet. "No, no, dear. Howard, I forbid you to put such nonsense into this child's head. You know how imaginative she is!"

"Yes, I know," he murmured, as if to himself; then he arose and held out both hands to the little girl.

"It's only a boy, Kittykins, who is poor and unhappy and in trouble, and whom I've promised to help. Dr. Fernald's going to show me how to do it, and I'm going down now to his house to find out about it."

CHAPTER 21

When the Reverend Doctor Fernald, pastor of a fashionable Fifth Avenue Church, lectured to his Men's Club on "The Juvenile Court," he did not know himself, perhaps, the extent of the forces he was putting into motion.

The club, laboriously gathered by the doctor from the men of his congregation, had for some time been a source of great anxiety and disappointment. He told himself that he realized, of course, that the club was composed mostly of either hard-headed men of business or light-hearted men of society and that he could not expect much from them. Yet he had hoped for—something. Thus far he had been disappointed. Doctrinal discourses plainly bored them. Political discussions fell flat. Social ethics, cults, and -isms of various sorts awakened only a fleeting impression. The club was plainly dwindling, both in numbers and in interest. Then one night he had spoken on "The Juvenile Court."

The change was electric. This was something new, something vital, something human; like one man, the club had responded. Before the lecture was a week old, each member had pledged himself to be a "Big Brother." Already the doctor had set ten of them at work, when he summoned Howard Preston.

Dr. Fernald had been a little fearful of Preston. He knew him as a young artist—rich, talented, popular, a little eccentric, and a member of one of the city's most exclusive families. He had been surprised when Preston joined the club, and he had been still more so when he received the young man's ready pledge to serve. If any lingering doubts remained in the doctor's mind, however, they faded quite away after one glance into Preston's eyes, when that young man called for "orders," as he expressed it.

"The boy's name is 'Marco Covino,'" began the doctor, characteristically going straight to the point. "He was up before the court last week for stealing scrap iron, and he's been turned over to us as a good subject for a 'Big Brother.' I've investigated his case somewhat, but I'll own I haven't found out much. He seems to be an odd chap and decidedly reserved."

"How old is he?"

"Fourteen. He lives with his father at the top of a tenement block in—I've forgotten the street, but I'll give you the address from my book. As near as I can judge, they have been moving from cellar to garret, and garret to cellar for the last two or three years. The man is sick."

"What is the trouble?"

"I should say, old-fashioned consumption—and drink. The boy sells papers, runs errands, blacks shoes, and does odd jobs of all sorts to bring in a little money. The man works only intermittently and drinks most of that up, I fancy. The boy was sullen and almost impertinent when he was brought before the court. Nobody could get much out of him. I've a shrewd suspicion that when we get to the bottom of the matter, we shall find out he stole for his father. I've been trying to trace his history, and though I didn't make out very well, I did find a city missionary, a Miss Dole, who knew him several years ago, but who had lost sight of him lately. She said he was a brave little chap then and doggedly devoted to his father. She declares that whatever he is now, she wouldn't hesitate to stake her faith in human nature on the real goodness of his heart—if one could ever get at the core under the crust that abuse, poverty, and hard luck have coated it with."

"And what am I to do?"

"You're to find that core," smiled the doctor, with a level look into the younger man's eyes.

Unconsciously, Preston straightened himself and squared his shoulders. He said nothing, and because he did say nothing the doctor was conscious of an odd gratification.

"You understand, of course," went on the doctor, after a moment, "that this isn't a charity scheme to give money. Aid of that sort is necessary sometimes, of course, and must be given. If you do find that it is needed now to any great extent, come to me, please, and we'll confer together, and with the association, and decide just how to go about it. But that doesn't reach the 'core,' you understand. Look the boy up; get acquainted with him. Find out what he likes and dislikes and how he spends his time. Help him to spend some of it yourself, perhaps. Take him home—to a good play—concert, or—or art exhibition," added the doctor, with a twinkle in his eye. "Take him to something you like. You can't be really interested in him, you know, unless he's interested in you. He must know what you like and what you do. In fact, he must find in you—if this thing is to be successful—a big brother."

"And he shall—God helping me!" cried Preston, rising to his feet.

"Good! And God will help you," returned the doctor, with a warm grip of his hand.

CHAPTER 22

It is one thing to march to war to the tune of "See, the Conquering Hero Comes," and with the ringing cheers of admiring throngs in one's ears; it is quite another thing to do picket duty on a lonely mountain at midnight with only the stars and silence for company.

In the doctor's study, with the doctor's stirring words in his ears, and with the club a full score strong at his back, Howard Preston counted success already his; but in the dark hallway at the top of a rickety stairway, and with fearsome snores coming from behind the door at which he was to knock, he saw failure staring him in the face. Yet Preston, even if he were the picket on the lonely mountain, was not the man to drop his gun and run. So, with a semblance of courage, he knocked at the door.

There was no answer.

He knocked again and waited.

There was still no answer.

At the third knock a door opened across the landing, and a frowzy head appeared.

"What you want?"

With the words came a fretful duet of wails from two children trying to peer around the woman's skirts, and over the woman's head floated out the aroma of rum, onions, and unwashed humanity.

The picket-man then did nearly drop his gun and run—nearly, but not quite.

"I'm looking for a boy named Marco Covino," said Preston pleasantly. "A man downstairs told me that the boy had just come up, but I have knocked several times and received no answer."

"Ho, that's nothin'," retorted the woman. "The boy doesn't answer knocks. He's afraid of police or Settlement folks; and his dad's asleep, likely, or drunk. If you want him, just open the door and walk in. He's there all right, I bet ye!"

"But—" Preston hesitated and stepped back. It had been his wish to come alone and try to make the boy's acquaintance. But he had not looked for such a reception as this; and, surely, to storm one's heart was no way to reach its core, he thought. The next moment he had no choice, however, for the owner of the frowzy head had stalked by him, banged the door open, and pushed him into the room with a swiftness and unexpectedness that left him literally gasping for breath.

"There!" she flung over her shoulder, as she retreated to her own quarters. "I reckon that'll teach him to answer a civil knock when he hears it!"

In the room Preston found himself confronting a dark-haired boy, who stood defiantly in the middle of the floor with a broken-nosed pitcher of water in both hands, ready to throw.

There was not a drawing-room, perhaps, in all of New York or London in which Preston would not have been at ease; but in the Covino attic he stood tongue-tied, staring helplessly at his young host.

The boy returned the gaze unflinchingly, for a time in silence; then he spoke, "If you come in any farther I'll let her drive—and it won't be just the water, neither. The jug'll go, too," he said quietly.

Preston laughed. For him the atmosphere had suddenly cleared.

"Well, I don't know as I blame you," he retorted, with a quietness that matched the boy's own. "One has to protect one's home from invasion some way, of course."

Marco's eyes widened. Unconsciously he lowered his weapon, but almost instantly he returned it to its old position, his eyes once more full of distrust.

"I'm not going," he announced, shortly.

"Where?"

"Anywheres—with you."

"Of course not! I didn't expect you would. Besides, I came here to see you."

Again the boy wavered, and again the old distrust plainly counseled caution. "Which be you, anyhow," he demanded, "police or Settlement folks?"

"Well, now, which do I look like?" asked Preston, with interest, much as if he had offered a challenge.

"There's no tellin'. There is cops what don't wear blue do's, and there is Settlement folks what don't wear glasses."

"Hmm, well, which do I act like?"

A faint twinkle crept into the boy's eyes. "There's no tellin' that, neither. There is freshies in all trades, you know."

Preston choked back a cough and raised his eyebrows. Then, with a complete change of manner, he turned, closed the door, and with easy nonchalance walked by the boy and the pitcher of water and sat down in a chair near the window.

"Hmm, well, it so happens that I'm neither the police nor a Settlement worker," he laughed. "So, as long as I'm not, perhaps you'll tell me just what it is you've got against those worthies, eh?"

It was a bold move. Preston himself, nonchalant as he appeared, was far from being confident of its success.

The boy stared, hesitated, then walked to the table and put down his pitcher of water. "Say, who be you, anyhow, and what did you come for?" he demanded.

Preston drew a long breath. He hoped his face did not show how great was his satisfaction.

"Well, my name is 'Preston'—'Howard Preston,' and I came—but suppose you tell me first what it is that you've got against the police and the Settlement people. It might be safer—for me, you know," he finished with an expressive smile.

To his joy the smile was answered, slowly, but unmistakably, in the gleam of appreciation that relaxed the boy's face. So elated, indeed, was the man that he plunged on recklessly.

"The police, now, what have they done?" he questioned. He saw his mistake at once in the angry flash that leaped to the dark eyes. "Or the Settlement people," he added, in hurried conciliation. "Suppose we begin with them. What have they done?"

"Nothin'."

"Oh, I thought they had. You seem not to like their—company."

"Well, they wanted me to leave Dad."

"They did?" Preston's voice expressed polite surprise. "Maybe they didn't understand just how the case stood. Anyhow, it wasn't very considerate of them, was it? Of course you wouldn't want to leave him!"

The boy turned quickly. The room was very quiet. Over in the corner the man still slept, but not so noisily. For a moment the boy gazed straight into his visitor's eyes. Into his own, the old distrust had sent a fierce gleam of suspicion.

"Look a-here, quit your chinnin," he snapped at last. "What do you want, anyhow?"

Preston laughed pleasantly. "I have been a good while coming to my errand, I'll own," he confessed. "The truth is, I'm painting a picture, and in it I'm putting a boy of just about your size. I need a model—a boy to look at, you know, so I'll be sure to get him in just right. I thought perhaps you'd be willing to come and pose for me—that is, just sit still and let me look at you while I paint. What do you say?"

There was no answer. The boy was dumb with sheer amazement.

"Of course you understand that I should pay you for your time," went on Preston, smoothly. "And I'm afraid I should need a good deal of it, too," he added, casually mentioning the sum per hour that his model might expect to receive.

The boy's eyes seemed almost to pop out of his head. "Ye don't mean that you'll pay me all that to just sit still and be looked at!" he exclaimed.

"Why, of course! You can't be earning anything anywhere else at the time, you know; and if I take you away from your regular employment, I should make good the time lost. Will that be enough to pay you for it, and will you come?"

The boy threw him a glance, half pitying, half scornful. "Oh yes, it's enough—and I'll come."

"Thank you," murmured Preston, and after giving explicit directions as to how, when, and where to go, he smilingly nodded his goodbye.

Once outside the stuffy hallways, he drew a deep breath. "I think I may say I've cracked the ice—if not broken it," he muttered to himself.

At home he told his mother this much, "Well, Mater, I went, I saw, and I think I conquered—at least to a certain extent. Anyway, the boy's promised to come up here tomorrow."

"Here? Oh, Howard, how could you—and so soon!"

"Don't worry, dear. It's only business—he thinks, I assure you. I'm going to paint him. He'll come to the studio like any other model. I'd keep Florence out of the way, however. I'm not quite ready yet for her to begin to be a 'sister' to him."

"Out of the way! I should say so," cried Mrs. Preston.

Her son smiled merrily as he turned to go upstairs. Ten minutes later he was busy making out the card that must go back to the executive secretary—his first report as a Big Brother.

CHAPTER 23

As the appointed hour for his new model's appearance drew near, Preston became more and more fearful that the boy would not come, after all. In the calm reasoning that the second day brought, his victory looked unpleasantly like defeat. He could not be at all positive now that the boy's last impish grin was not a sure indication that the whole thing had been to him a huge joke and that he had agreed to the arrangement merely to rid himself of a troublesome visitor. Great was Preston's sorrow, therefore—but not his surprise—when the boy failed to appear.

Afternoon found Preston once more at the top of the rickety tenement-house stairs. This time he knocked and spoke just as he gently pushed open the door.

"They said you were up here, so I came right in," he began, briskly. "I didn't want to be mistaken for anybody I wasn't, this time, you see. Besides, I wanted to make sure I found you. I'm afraid my directions weren't clear somehow yesterday. You didn't come this morning."

"No, I didn't come." The boy was alone in the room, sitting in a chair by the window. He did not even turn his head as he spoke.

"Get lost?"

A fleeting something like derision crossed the boy's face. "No, I didn't go."

"Oh, come now! You know I engaged you, and—"

"I had another job—Dad," interrupted the boy, abruptly.

"Oh, I see. Sick?"

"No, drunk."

There was a momentary pause. Preston was uncertain just how to proceed. His eyes were on the defiantly up-tilted chin opposite. To his surprise, the boy himself made the next move. Had Preston but known it, the lonely little fellow had reached the point where human sympathy—even though from a stranger—seemed an absolute necessity.

"Ye see, Dad was down to Sullivan's, cuttin' up like time, and they come for me," he explained, with a quivering that contradicted the defiant chin. "There isn't anybody what can do so much with Dad as I can, most generally. But even I wasn't no use this time."

"Why, what happened?"

"He ran off—got away. I don't know where he is. I came home; I thought maybe he'd be here."

"Oh, he'll come back all right, never fear."

"But he's sick."

"All the more reason why you'll see him, then. He won't stay away long."

The boy turned fiercely.

"Maybe now you want me to leave him! Eh?"

"By no means," retorted the man, promptly. "But see here, we are quite forgetting what I came for, and there's my picture waiting for its model—and all because you didn't come this morning."

A faint ray of interest came into the boy's eyes. "Say, did you mean it—all that chinnin' about my bein' paid for bein' looked at?"

"Certainly. I engaged you, too, though not in writing. I don't believe, however, that you're the sort of boy that goes back on his word just because he hasn't signed his name."

Unconsciously the boy lifted his chin a little. The man saw the movement and smiled.

"Of course you couldn't come this morning," he went on, smoothly. "More important duties detained you. But I fancy you'll be there tomorrow morning all right."

"Sure, I'll be there tomorrow mornin'," promised the boy, decidedly. And Preston went home well content.

In the studio of the Preston mansion the next morning, the arrival of the new model was awaited with much interest. Preston had wanted to stay longer with the boy the day before, but something within him had warned him that Marco would be quick to resent anything that savored of intrusion into his own affairs, and the new Big Brother did not wish to jeopardize, by too much haste, the little success that he had already won. So he had steeled himself to come away.

By Preston's orders, the boy was shown directly to the studio. He came in with an air of timidity that was yet half bravado. When Preston caught sight of him, he was mimicking the pompous footman behind his back, and so perfectly that Preston had difficulty to keep his face as he advanced with outstretched hand.

"Good morning, Marco. I'm glad to see you're so prompt."

"Gee, but isn't he swell!" murmured the boy, his eyes following the retreating form of the livery-clad servant. "Isn't it all swell!" he finished, his admiring gaze sweeping the sumptuous room.

"I'm glad you like it," laughed the artist. "You see, if you're to spend so much time here sitting for me, you will want something pleasant to look at, and—" He stopped in surprise. A curious light had come to the boy's face. His eyes were on an enormous landscape that covered almost half the wall space across the room. As if fascinated, he was creeping with soundless steps nearer and nearer to the painting, his gaze never leaving it. Then instinctively he began to move backward—he had gone too near for the best effect. At just the right point he stopped and fell softly to one knee, his hand shading his eyes, as if he were out of doors in the sunlight.

"Why, Mister, it's trees and grass and sky," he breathed, in an awestruck voice.

"Thank you," murmured the picture's creator.

"And there's water there, too," continued the boy, rapturously. "Why, Mister, it don't seem as if it could be just—" He stopped and rose to his feet. With almost reverent hesitation he advanced close to the painting, then turned sharply. "It is! It isn't only painted!"

"Thank you," murmured the artist again, strangely moved.

The boy had gone back to his old position, his eyes aflame.

"I don't see how you did it," he muttered, as if to himself. "They are real trees and grass and sky—they is."

"Thank you. I'm glad you like the picture," said Preston, tremulously.

There was a moment's pause, then he spoke again.

"But how is it that you know so much about them—trees and grass and sky? Where you live—you don't have them there, do you?"

"I reckon I don't," retorted the boy, almost chokingly. "Seems sometimes as if I never did have 'em. But I did! I had them last at that there place, Mont-Lawn, up the river. And it was like that, too," he added, turning absorbedly to the picture. "A great big place where you could breathe, with water 'way off. I used to set and look at it. It was there, you know, where I found out about bein' red, white, and blue to Dad."

"You found out about being—what?"

"About bein' red, white, and blue to dad, you know," repeated the boy, his dreamy eyes still on the picture.

There was a dazed silence; then dimly the man understood. With a sudden impulse he held out his hand. "Good for you, Marco!" he cried, unsteadily. "And I'm glad to meet a boy who's red, white, and blue like that!"

CHAPTER 24

The new model came three times a week to the studio. The acquaintance was progressing surely, but slowly—altogether too slowly for Preston's satisfaction. The man had looked for it to go by leaps and bounds after that illuminating scene before the picture on that first day; great was his disappointment to find that Marco kept himself most of the time fast locked in a reserve that admitted scant chance for intimacy.

So eager was Preston to gain the boy's confidence that sometimes he went too far, and he had to beat a hasty retreat that would yet cover the real purpose of the attack.

The boy was a puzzle to him. To Dr. Fernald, Preston owned that he had never known such a mixture of good and evil, of traits lovable and unlovable, of honesty and dishonesty. The heart was there—Preston had not forgotten that first day in the studio—but it seemed hopelessly encased in an armor that defied the most-carefully pointed darts, and Preston was at times almost ready to give up in despair.

The boy was very punctual at the studio. He frankly liked the work—and the pay for it. He admired the pictures and spent long absorbed minutes before the great landscape across the room, but never again did any of them stir him out of himself as had that same landscape stirred him on that first day.

In his ideas on money matters the boy was, perhaps, the greatest enigma to Preston. Charity he refused outright. He was honesty itself when it came to paying his just debts—but he reveled in craps and marbles and dice-throwing for money at every opportunity;

the rights of property-holders were respected by him only to the extent of his inability to get possession of any object he desired. He scrupulously paid to Preston the five cents he had borrowed for car fare—and that same day a dollar bill disappeared from the studio, obviously by no other hand than his.

When Preston, somewhat at a loss how to proceed, questioned the boy as to his opinion of pilfering in general, he received a reply that disconcerted him not a little.

"It seems to me," the boy explained, "that what's lyin' round loose belongs to anyone what is smart enough to get it first. Course, what you owe and promise to pay is different; that isn't yours—you've given it away already. But when it comes to other stuff, why, that belongs to whoever gets it first and is smart enough to keep it. Besides, there's Dad; it isn't often that just what money I earn'll take care of him, and I has to take what I can git. Of course, Dad's got to be looked out for!"

Preston knew then that the secret of the scrap iron stealing was his—and he knew something else, too: he knew that the task Dr. Fernald had given him to do was even harder than either of them had thought it to be.

Very cautiously, Preston set to work to change the boy's method of reasoning. Bit by bit he endeavored to give him new standards of right and wrong. And through it all, he tried to be just and gentle and patient. He remembered the boy's life and surroundings and his struggle for very existence. But he wondered, sometimes, as the days passed, if he were accomplishing much, after all.

There was one thing, however, that he had accomplished. February was nearly gone now, and Preston had won the boy's promise to go into school the first of March, when the picture would be finished. Even this would not have been possible, however, but for the fact of one other victory; and this victory, Preston sometimes thought, was the most significant of all: "Dad" was going away.

For some weeks now, John Covino had been at home, half drunk, half crazy, wholly a very terror to the boy who did not swerve from the most devoted attendance. Preston had for some time had in mind an institution that he knew of, half way between a sanatorium and a reformatory, where Covino could be well cared for and where he might possibly regain health and strength. Preston had told the boy of this place and had glowingly set forth its advantages, using every argument in his power to gain the boy's approval. Just how he had finally won it, however, he did not himself understand until Marco, in his own words, explained it.

"Ye see, it isn't as if I was leavin' Dad. I wouldn't do that, course; and you know it. But it's Dad what's leavin' me. And that's all right, 'cause he'll be better off, and be took care of, and get well and strong. And it isn't charity, neither, exactly, 'cause you say Dad can work himself when he's well enough, and pay his way. Of course, you know Dad and me wouldn't want no charity!" And so the matter was settled, much to Preston's relief and delight.

Preston's friends laughed sometimes over his absorption in his new work, but Preston only smiled in return. He was not ready to talk. Mrs. Preston sighed and shook her head over his "infatuation," and sometimes she pleaded with him. To her Preston spoke earnestly, at times, of his hopes and plans—though not often. On one thing, however, they were agreed: Florence must not see the boy. He was certainly no fit companion for her—yet, Preston said. And as Florence was in school and had her own interests, and as the studio was quite apart from the rest of the house, this exclusion of interaction was easily accomplished.

In March, John Covino went away, and Marco began school again. Marco lived now with a family whom Preston had found and who were glad to board the boy in return for light work that he could do out of school hours. He came to the studio now only Saturday mornings, but Preston still saw him often during the week. Preston understood that it must not be all elimination in the case of this young brother of his—it must be equally implantation. Where he strove to take away an interest that was evil, he must have ready to replace it one that was good; and to that end, he loaned the boy books and magazines, introduced him into a good gymnasium, took him to vesper service once or twice, and finally persuaded him to join a boys' club, at the head of which was Dr. Fernald himself.

It was in March, on a particularly warm Saturday, that he invited the boy to go for a ride in his motor-car, and to them both that ride was a revelation.

On this occasion, Preston was his own chauffeur, and, as he expected, every throb of the engine and every turn of the wheel were of entrancing interest to the boy at his side; but all this lost its attraction when the wide sweep of open country was reached.

They were far up on the beautiful river road. The green of the hills and of the trees was only a promise of what it would be, but the sun shone, the water rippled and glistened, and the broad blue sky was over all. To Marco's face came a glorified light that made Preston silent with amazement. Instinctively, he lessened his speed and brought the car almost to a stop. In the boy's eyes he had discovered the look that he had seen there once before and that he had so longed to see again—the look that had been in them on that first day in the studio.

"Gee, Mr. Preston, isn't it going to be great out here by and by," murmured the boy. "Isn't it great now!"

"It certainly is, Marco."

"Back there, sometimes, I 'most forget there is such places," continued the boy dreamily, "and then I remember Mont-Lawn, and I know there is."

"Mont-Lawn?"

"Yes. It's a place up the river where they take kids and give them ten days in the country. They let you sing and stay outdoors all day; and they tell you about—about God and flags, and—and being red, white, and blue, you know. It isn't hard to be that, neither, when you've got all this 'round ye—trees and grass and sky. Why, seems to me, sometimes, if I had it—like this, you know—I could be red, white, and blue to—to everybody!"

Preston's heart leaped, and his eyes grew misty; but he only said, in a carefully matter-of-fact voice, "I'm going camping, Marco, in June, and I'm thinking maybe I'll take you along with me, if you'd like to go. It'll be all grass and trees and sky there. Will you go?"

And in the boy's ecstatic sigh of content the man was answered.

CHAPTER 25

Marco was spending Saturday afternoon at the studio, just a week after the automobile ride. A new picture was being planned, and Preston was posing his model in different positions when Mrs. Preston came hurriedly into the room.

"Oh, I beg your pardon," she murmured hastily. "I thought you had finished—it is so late."

"We had practically finished. We were just talking. What is it, Mother? You look disturbed."

"I am disturbed—seriously. Morenski has sent word that he can't come tonight."

"Then we'll have to do without him, I suppose," smiled the man.

Mrs. Preston lifted her head impatiently.

"But, Howard, don't you see? There are guests—and he was my bright particular star for the evening. The rest are all well enough, so far as they go, but alone they'd make a slim program for such a musicale as people expect this to be. It was cruel of Morenski to treat me like this and to spoil things so! And there's the duchess and all her party—and you know how she adores the violin!"

"But isn't there someone else? Surely, in all New York there ought to be some fiddler you could get!"

Mrs. Preston gave her son a scornful glance.

"'Fiddler!' That's just about what I'd get," she retorted, mournfully, "at this late day and so late in the season, too! But I did try. I've telephoned everywhere. I even tried to get another instrument. I don't want a singer; I have enough of those. But I couldn't get a thing—that I'd take, of course. Howard, what shall I do?"

Preston started to speak, but to his surprise Marco stepped eagerly forward.

"Was it someone to play the fiddle that you wanted?" he questioned.

"Why, y-yes." Mrs. Preston was too amazed to say more.

"Well, that's all right then. I can do that for you."

"You can—do—that—for me!" In her stupefaction Mrs. Preston could scarcely articulate the words. But in a moment she found her temper and her voice, both at once. "Do you mean to say, boy, that you would come before my guests tonight and play—for me?" she demanded.

"Sure I would," returned Marco promptly, entirely misconstruing her meaning. "I'd do that, and more for you. Mr. Preston here has been mighty good to me, and there isn't anythin' I wouldn't do for him and you!"

Mrs. Preston fell limply back in her chair. She could not speak. The boy waited impatiently, his eyes alight. At last Preston cleared his throat.

"But, Marco, do you quite understand—do you think you could—" He paused, helplessly. A curious something in the boyish face opposite had stayed the words on his lips. The next moment he crossed the room and took from a closet a violin in its case. "I happen to have a violin here that I used to play myself a bit," he said. "Suppose you play a little for us now, Marco," he suggested, as steadily as he could. "Suppose you show us just what you can—do."

"Howard! Howard!" remonstrated Mrs. Preston, feebly.

If the boy heard her, he did not seem to understand. To the amazement of both the man and the woman, he opened the case, took out the violin, and began with a practiced hand to prepare it for use. They noticed that he handled it lovingly, with tender fingers; but at the first long-drawn note of sweetness, they both came suddenly erect in their chairs.

If Marco had understood what was at stake, he could scarcely have done better. The violin was a rare one, a genuine Cremona. He did not know that, it is true, but he did know that in it he was finding music that was rare indeed. In five minutes he had lost himself in his playing, as he always did when he was deeply stirred.

Save for the music, the room was breathlessly still. Over in the west the sun dropped out of sight, and the shadows deepened, but the man and the woman did not stir until, with a long sigh of ecstasy, the boy stopped playing.

"Gee! That fiddle's great," he breathed.

Mrs. Preston sprang to her feet and held out both her hands.

"Boy, boy, do you know what you are?" she cried. "You're wonderful! You're a genius! Of course you'll play tonight! And you'll play just as you are, and we'll have the room darkened like this. You'll be 'The Minstrel of the Streets.' Oh, Howard, won't it be lovely! Howard, why don't you say something?"

"Because I—can't, Mother," laughed the man, a bit unsteadily. "After all, perhaps you've—said it."

When Mrs. Preston had left the room, her son turned to the boy, who was still tenderly fingering the violin. "Who taught you to play like that, Marco?" he asked.

"Mumsey, first. After that I just played. Then, two years ago, there was an old man what lived where we did, and he played bang-up, he did—in orchestras, and all that. He taught me pieces—lots of 'em, nicer 'n mine, you know, like this." And there floated out into the room the first sweet tones of the ever-familiar, ever-beautiful "Intermezzo" from Cavalleria Rusticana.

For some time after the peculiarly haunting strains had died into silence, Preston sat motionless; then he lifted his head.

"But how does it happen that you never played before—to me?" he questioned.

The boy's face hardened.

"I haven't played much for the past year—until just lately. You see, Dad—well, Dad made me play for his drinks, or else to get the money to buy them with; and I got so that I—I hated it so much." The boy hesitated, then went on fiercely. "Of course, Dad had a right to do it. I was his, and if he wanted me to, I ought to have done it. But I didn't like to play—that way."

"Well, no, I should say not," affirmed Preston grimly. Then he added, with brisk cheeriness, "But now, suppose you play again to me, so that we may decide just what we'll play tonight. By the way, we'll have dinner here in the studio—just you and I—then you'll be here all ready for this evening, without having to go home."

"Jiminy, won't that be great!" exulted Marco, as he raised his violin again to his chin. "Maybe you'd like this now," he suggested. "It's kind of slow like that 'ere 'Intermezzer' what the man taught me." And he began to play.

The room was almost dark now. In the corner, Preston scarcely breathed, so weirdly sweet was the melody that came out of the shadows where Marco stood. When the last strain had ceased, Preston drew a rapturous sigh.

"Good heavens, boy! And to think you've had all this locked up within you, and I didn't even guess it! What was that piece?"

"Did you like it, really?" rejoiced Marco. "I like the slow ones, too, but most folks don't. They want the jigs what goes fast, most generally."

"Liked it? Of course I liked it! But what was it?"

"It's nothing, really, you know. That is, it isn't printed on paper like real pieces. I only made it up long ago. It's 'Lost on the Ocean Wave.'"

"You made it up! 'Lost on the Ocean Wave!'"

"Yes. I made up the music, and Flossie made up the name. She liked it so much—that piece."

"Who's Flossie?"

"My sister."

"Why, have you a sister Flossie, too? So have I."

"You have?—A sister Flossie, like me?" cried Marco.

"Well, her name is 'Florence,' and she isn't really a sister, I suppose," admitted the man. "But we call her that. She has been in our family several years, and we all love her very dearly."

"But you have your sister, and I haven't. I lost her ages and ages ago," mourned Marco.

The man caught the sob in the boy's voice and thought he understood: the little girl was dead, probably. He would remember and would be very careful not to grieve the boy again by speaking of her. He would be sure, too, that he did not say much about their own little Florence. It might bring sad memories. Before he could speak and answer the boy, however, the door opened, and Mrs. Preston's voice cried in surprise:

"In the dark still?"

"Yes," laughed Preston, as he stepped to the switch and turned on the electric lights. "Fortunately, our young artist here isn't confined to his notes."

"Of course he isn't, the dear child! And that's all the better for my plans," cried Mrs. Preston. "Howard, I've the loveliest idea for his numbers! Come, I want to show it to you. We'll be back in a moment, my dear," she nodded to Marco, as she left the room. To her son she said:

"I'm a little disturbed about Florence. She wants to sit up this evening and hear the music. But I can't let her, of course. It'll be so late—and you know how excitable and nervous she is. I did right in saying no. Don't you think so?" she concluded anxiously.

"I do," agreed the man with decision.

"I told her she might leave her door open after she'd gone to bed, and then she could hear the music almost the same."

"Of course," rejoined the man. "That is much the better way."

CHAPTER 26

The great Preston mansion was ablaze with lights from basement to roof. Outside, a crawling line of carriages and motor-cars extended far down the avenue. Inside, the perfume of flowers, the flash of jewels, and the swish of silken draperies, together with the sound of gay voices and soft laughter, told that Mrs. Preston's musicale was to be a success, at least so far as the size and brilliancy of the audience were concerned. The far-famed, much-sought-after duchess with her party had arrived and had been given the place of honor.

Everywhere there was an undercurrent of half-subdued excitement. Something was in the air—something mysterious and delightful. Morenski was not coming; everyone knew that—and everyone was disappointed. Yet with the disappointment came a curious elation. There was to be something—somebody to take his place—a surprise. And most of the guests knew Mrs. Preston and her "surprises" of old—they awaited this one with eagerness.

Finally, the last motor-car crept to the door, the last silken drapery swished into silence—and the music began.

There was a piano solo, perfunctorily played and perfunctorily applauded. Then a male quartet appeared the applause swelled to an encore this time. The third number on the program aroused a great deal of enthusiasm. It was a song by a diva noted for her beauty, her voice, and for the almost prohibitory price that she set on her services for an occasion like this. It was known, indeed, that only one other—the absent Morenski—was more difficult to obtain.

One by one the artists appeared, made their bow, and retired only to reappear later; and still tantalizing suspense hovered over the politely listening guests. Then came a pause—so long a pause that the eager hum of voices unconsciously hushed itself into silence.

Suddenly the audience became aware that the lights were growing dim. Breathlessly the throng watched until the great music-room was almost in darkness, save where a startled eye or a flashing jewel caught a gleam from some half-hidden electric light. The silence grew more intense as every gaze turned toward the slowly parting curtains that hung before the great alcove window at the end of the room. Then a long-drawn "O-oh!" of delight swept the throng, and Mrs. Preston knew that she had won.

In the alcove, every blind and shade and curtain had been removed, leaving the great plate-glass windows on all sides free and clear. The music-room was at the top of the house, and the windows looked out on a far-reaching sky which was just now a huge half-dome of velvety blue-gray, flecked with stars and hung with the silver disk of the moon. In the alcove, with the moonlight full upon him, stood a boy, thin-faced and ill-clad, with a violin at his chin, a voice from somewhere announced, "The Minstrel of the Streets," and the boy began to play.

Downstairs a certain little girl, who had tried very hard to keep awake, heard the first strains and drowsily blinked her eyes. For some time, she listened rapturously. It was beautiful music, and on it she seemed to float away—away—far up into the sky, where the stars and the angels were; away—away—and she did float away, quite away to sleep, long before the playing had ceased.

In the music-room there was the rapt silence of amazed appreciation. According to the prearranged plan, Marco was passing from one piece to another much as he liked to play when alone. So far as Marco himself was concerned, indeed, he was alone. He knew, to be sure, that in the room before him there were men and women listening. But he had not seen them, and they only loomed now ghostlike out of the shadows. Besides, he had half turned so that he might look out of the window at the moon and the far-away stars, and he was playing to them. He finished, in accordance with Preston's suggestion, with "Lost on the Ocean Wave."

As the last strains quivered into silence, there was the supreme tribute of a breathless hush; then the applause burst like a thunderclap, and a storm of excited voices swept through the room. The next instant the lights flashed on, and a dark-eyed, dark-haired, very much embarrassed boy looked around for the nearest means of escape.

Marco had been greatly distressed from the first over his clothes. He regretted exceedingly that Mrs. Preston insisted on his wearing the ragged suit in which he posed for her son. His own garments, worn every day, were poor enough, certainly, he thought; but they would have been infinitely better than these rags. He felt now worse than ever to be in the bright light, and with those richly-dressed men and women all staring at him and clapping their hands. He decided to get away at once; and with that end in view, he made a dive for the nearest door. But his old expertness in dealing with crowds must have deserted him, for he promptly found himself entangled in a cloud of spangled tulle that seemed to float around a very pretty young lady who was holding out both her hands to him, and exclaiming, "Oh—you—dear!"

A long hour afterward, Preston found the boy hiding behind one of the pictures in the darkest corner of the studio.

"Well, my boy, you may come out now," he laughed.

"Are they gone?" Marco's eyes were wide and cautious.

"All gone."

"Gee, but they were corkers!" cried the boy, stiffly crawling from his hiding-place. "Why, they hugged me—hugged me!—those women did."

Preston chuckled, but he answered gravely, "They liked your music, Marco."

"And they trim flowers at me, and smoothed my hair, an'—and kissed me, Mr. Preston. They kissed me!"

The man laughed.

"I'm afraid you don't half appreciate your blessings," he said. "There's many a man who would give much for one of those kisses you scorned."

"Huh? Well, maybe," admitted Marco, doubtfully. "But I wouldn't."

Half an hour later came the end of that wonderful day—an end so marvelous that Marco quite pinched himself to make sure he was awake. Beside no less a personage than the Preston chauffeur, and in no less a vehicle than the Preston motor-car, he made the journey to the humble little home where he worked for his board.

CHAPTER 27

There was great excitement in the world—the world of Mrs. Preston's musicale—and there was little talked of but Mrs. Preston's "find." The boy was undoubtedly wonderfully gifted—a genius, in fact; upon that all were agreed. The only question now remaining was, how should this great talent be best developed?

Suggestions were not wanting. The Prestons were besieged with them. Philanthropists offered uncounted money, and music instructors placed at Preston's disposal unlimited service. Everywhere were to be found men of wealth and women of fashion who had some plan to propose. Even the duchess signified her gracious willingness to take the boy abroad and place him under the best masters. And at all of it, Preston only smiled and bowed his thanks, with an apologetic, "It has not been decided yet just what he will do."

At last, however, there came a plan that made Preston pause and think. For some days he pondered it; then he summoned Marco to the studio.

"Well, my boy," he began, cheerily, "I've some good news for you. Dr. Fernald sails next week for Europe. He will have with him his wife and his son, about your age. They will travel for a few months, and they invite you to go with them; then in September they will place you where you can obtain the best possible instruction on the violin and make an artist of yourself."

"Do you mean I can get to be a player like granddad and earn money concerting and all that?"

"Yes, I'm sure you can. Will you go?"

"Go! I just reckon I—but there's Dad!" The boy's face fell, and his eyes grew anxious.

"But your father is well off where he is, and you could do nothing if you stayed. Besides, I'm here, and I'll look after him and be sure he is well taken care of. Now will you go?"

"You just bet I will!" breathed the boy.

"There's something else to it, too, Marco, that's particularly fine for you. In Dr. Fernald's party, there will be a young college fellow who is going partly for his health. You will be his especial charge, and you are to study with him four hours every day. You know schools have been few and far between with you, and you want to know something besides music."

"Yes, I know," murmured Marco abstractedly. (Marco was still in the promised land of September with his violin.) "And will that fiddle-man learn me pieces, real pieces printed on paper, same as the old man did?"

"Yes." And Preston launched into a glowing description of what the future surely held for him, if he would but do his best—a description so altogether delightful that Marco went home as in a dream. Yet only the next day Preston received a note laboriously written in Marco's best hand.

"Deer sir. I cant go. Good by Your Friend MARCO."

In less than an hour, Preston was confronting a wistful-faced boy, whose eyes were sad, but whose chin was determined.

"Why, Marco, what's up?" he demanded.

"I can't go."

"Why not?"

"The folks here say it'll cost an awful lot to do all that, and I don't have the money to pay."

"Of course you haven't, but I attend to that part."

"You mean you pay it?"

"Yes."

The boyish form drew itself suddenly erect.

"Thank you, but I can't take it. I'm not one to take charity."

"Of course not," retorted Preston, with a promptness that he hoped was prompt enough. "It's merely a loan, you know. You may pay me back when you like."

A dawning hope came into the somber eyes.

"You mean—" began the boy, eagerly; then the hope fled and left a dull weariness. "I owe already eight dollars and forty cents to Mis' Martin where I come from. I reckon I better not get into debt no more till that is paid," he finished, disconsolately.

Preston coughed, to hide the smile he could not restrain.

"But you don't understand," he urged, gravely. "All this is merely to put you in a position where you can pay the—the eight dollars and forty cents. When you learn to play well enough, you'll find people will pay you a great deal of money for your services. It's merely this: I believe in you; I'm willing to take the risk. I'll pay for your musical education, and when it's yours, you may turn around and pay me back, if you like. See—just a straight business proposition!"

"'Just a straight business proposition,'" echoed the boy, hope growing larger and larger in his eyes. "Say, I reckon I will do it!" he finished, with a sudden whoop of joy. And Preston knew that the battle was won.

Six days later, Preston stood on the pier and waved a long goodbye to his "brother." The man's eyes were moist. He wondered if, after all, he had ever come near the "core." Whether he had or not, he reflected, there could be no better hands in which to leave his uncompleted work than those of Dr. Fernald, the man who now stood by the boy's side.

On the deck of the great steamship, at that moment, Marco was watching with swimming eyes the white speck that stood for Preston's handkerchief on the fast-receding shore.

"Jiminy!" he was muttering under his breath. "The feller what wouldn't be red, white, and blue to him—and to anybody else he wants him to be—wouldn't be worth a—a tow string for a fiddle!

CHAPTER 28

On a beautiful day in February, a little less than eight years after Preston had waved a goodbye to Marco, the man stood once more on the pier, this time to welcome a very pretty girl with a fluff of yellow hair under her smart traveling hat.

"Florence!"

"Howard!" she greeted him joyfully. "I thought you'd be here. And Mother?"

"She couldn't come—a sprained ankle—nothing serious, dear," he added quickly, at her look of alarm. "But you—how well you are looking! The trip has done you good!"

"Yes, I think it has," she smiled, coloring a little at the ardent admiration in the man's eyes. "But, come, let us hurry through with the baggage and with my goodbyes to the Batons. I want to get home to—Mother."

She hesitated a moment before the last word, and the man turned quickly. There was a question in his eyes, but he only said, quietly, "All right—and she'll want to see you, too."

In the motor-car, some time later, they picked their way through the heterogeneous mass of humanity and vehicles in the crowded streets and turned into the wider avenue that led toward home. The way was clearer now, but still all of Preston's attention was needed to guide the car, and the eager question that his eyes still held remained unspoken. It was not until after dinner, indeed, when Preston found himself for the first time really alone with the girl, that the question reached his lips.

"Florence, that hesitation just a moment before the 'mother'—did it mean—anything?" he asked, in a voice that shook a little.

A quick shadow of distress crossed the girl's face. "No, no, Howard, please don't," she begged. "I know I hesitated, and I could have shaken myself the next moment. I knew you'd see it, and—and think things. And you did."

"But, you see, it means so much—to me."

"But it mustn't! It wasn't anything. Don't you see?" urged the girl, feverishly. "It's only that now I—I'm conscious all the time of my position, and that—that she isn't my mother."

"But—I want her to be—your mother."

A swift red flew to the girl's face.

"I know, and she is—that is, she was. And I want her to be—as she was—only—Howard, you know what I mean!"

"I'm afraid I do," he returned sadly, "but I thought—I hoped—Florence, dear, haven't these three long months brought any change?"

She shook her head, but as the quick pain leaped to the other's eyes, she said hurriedly, "That is, I can't be sure yet. You know three months is so short to—to decide." She broke off in sudden animation. "Howard, I found Madge Dana in Paris, and she's just lovely. I've invited her to come to us in June. I'm just sure you'll like her!"

In spite of the pang that her words gave him, Preston laughed outright. His eyes, however, carried no smile as he spoke.

"Florence, do you know, dear, that's the most hopeless word you have given me? Girls who are in love, or almost in love, are not so anxious to introduce a possible rival."

"But I didn't—that is—Howard, I don't love you that way," cried the girl, desperately. "Don't you see it's all so different? You've been my big brother—my adored big brother, all these years. And I—I never thought of anything else until that night three months ago, just before I sailed, and you—told me. I've tried to think, to plan it out, to weigh it in my mind, ever since; but it wasn't the kind of thing you can think out and plan and weigh. Seems to me, if it's love, that kind of love, it will just—just come, and I shall know it. And maybe it will come now. I have loved you dearly, as a brother, ever since I was a little girl, and it doesn't seem as if it would be hard for the other to grow out of it. I hope it will grow—truly I do," she added earnestly. But at the eager movement of the man opposite, she drew back. "Let us leave things just as they were, please," she implored, "and then see if it will—will grow. Don't ask me—don't talk of it, not for a while, please. And don't speak of it to your mother. Surely you'll do that—for my sake?"

"I surely will—and more, if I can," promised the man, holding out both his hands. "'Given under my hand—and seal,'" he finished softly, as he bent and kissed her fingers.

CHAPTER 29

Mrs. Preston did not appear at the breakfast table on the morning after Florence's arrival. The night before, with the aid of her son's arm, she had gone down to dinner; but the doctor had strongly advised caution and little activity, and so she kept rather closely to her rooms. It was a tête-à-tête breakfast, therefore, for her son and Florence; and the girl, determined to strike at once the desired note of unembarrassed friendliness, began cheerily, after the coffee was poured:

"And now tell me about yourself, Howard. What have you been doing, and what are you doing now?"

Preston, true to his promise, was quick to respond to her overture.

"I'm afraid there's little to tell of interest," he replied. "The most exciting thing, to me, that I know of just now, is the expected arrival in New York of a young friend of mine—Marco Covino."

"The violinist—and the boy you helped years ago!"

"How did you know anything about that part, I should like to know," retorted Preston.

"Not from you, certainly, Sir Modesty," laughed the girl, with a playful toss of her head. "But 'there are others,' you know! Besides, it was only eight years ago, and I remember something myself about a mysterious boy to whom you were being a 'Big Brother.' I think perhaps I should have been more curious, only I was a tiny bit jealous. I didn't relish your being 'Big Brother' to anyone but me. But tell me about him," she hurried on, suddenly realizing that their own brotherly and sisterly relationship was not the subject she wished to discuss just then. "Tell me what you know of this man—everyone knows the other part, of course, since he's become so famous."

"That's exactly it," retorted Preston, with mock dismay. "It's because he has become so famous that I'm so excited and so—er—uncertain. I'm like the hen with the duckling, and my duckling has set sail on such high seas of fame and prosperity that I can't do anything but run back and forth on the bank and wonder what it is all about, anyway."

"Oh, Howard, Howard!" laughed the girl. "You don't always use a brush when you paint a picture, do you?"

"But it's really so," declared Preston, earnestly. "Eight years ago, when he left me, he was a raw, slangy boy with eyes that carried alternately the most adorable dreaminess and the most reprehensible—mischief, to put it mildly. And now—"

"And now," supplemented Florence quickly, "he comes back a man—grown, polished, famous, and with a heart of pure gold."

A glad light sprang to Preston's eyes. "How do you know—that last?" he demanded. "Who told you?"

"Mrs. Fernald. You know she is in Paris again this winter. I saw her. Oh, I know something about this protégé of yours, after all," she teased, merrily. Then her eyes suddenly softened. "And I know, too, who is responsible for it all—yourself," she finished.

"I? Why, I haven't seen the boy for eight years. I just missed him both in Paris and Berlin when I was there, and you know I was called home suddenly."

"But you saw a great deal of him before, here in New York," reminded the girl. "Mrs. Fernald told me all about that first trip which he took with them, how tractable he was, how earnestly he studied with his tutor, and how hard he tried to improve in every way. She said they found out, after a time, that it was all because of you. It was something you said to him just before he sailed, and he said he was trying to do it: he was trying to be red, white, and blue to you, to himself, and to—God."

The girl's voice broke a little, and there was a moment's pause. Across the table the man did not speak. He was too deeply moved for words.

"And so that was the secret of it," resumed the girl softly. "And you can imagine that the good doctor did not let your work go untended and unwatched. He was always there to help and to guide, as only Dr. Fernald knew how to help and guide, in such cases. He never told you all this, perhaps, for he hardly had the chance, as he died so soon after that trip, while still abroad. But the boy—surely he wrote you sometimes?"

Preston smiled oddly. "Oh, yes, he wrote me—after a fashion; but he was nearly always reserved in his speech, and still more so with his pen; and about his real self he wrote little. I have kept his letters. Taken from first to last, they are a most illuminating commentary on his progress, if nothing more. I took out the first and the last one this morning to look at them. Perhaps you would like to see them—as a study in contrasts," he suggested, taking from his pocket two letters and handing them across the table. And Florence read first:

"Deer sir. I'm having a Bully time. How far down does this Water go. Good by. Your Friend MARCO."

The second letter, after the preliminaries of date and address, was:

"Dear Mr. Preston: I sail the tenth from Cherbourg on the Caspian. Aside from my father's, there is just one man's face in all America that I am longing to see—yours.

"As ever, with the most heartfelt appreciation of all you have done for me, I am,

"Faithfully yours,

"Marco Covino."

"What a strong, fine hand he writes!" mused the girl, admiringly. Then, with a mischievous smile, she demanded: "Do you realize, sir, what it would mean to countless autograph hunters to get a letter with that signature? Why, that man is the idol of half of Europe and bids fair to be of this country as well."

"Yes, I know," returned Preston, uncomfortably. "That's where the duckling comes in."

Florence laughed.

"But are his letters always so short and to the point?" she asked.

"Usually. Oh, of course, there have been longer ones. For instance, from the first he insisted that Dr. Fernald should keep a strict account of what was paid out for him, and he was equally careful to do so for himself, later on. With the first money he earned, he began to pay me back. The letters about that time were longer, of course."

"And is he—er—out of debt now?"

"Entirely, so far as I am concerned," replied Preston, with a whimsical smile. "I believe there is a matter of eight dollars and forty cents which he still owes to a Mrs. Martin, somewhere. He sent me an elaborate explanation at the first to the effect that, although this eight dollars and forty cents was the older debt, he did not intend to pay it until he returned to this country."

"'Eight dollars and forty cents'! —and the great Covino!" exclaimed Florence. "What a bundle of contradictions that man must be! I long to meet him. And you say he has paid you all back?"

"Yes," rejoined the man. "As was natural, I suppose, with such talent, he responded to instruction with a promptness that very soon placed him on the road to really great playing. Of course, that sort of thing couldn't be hid, and it was not long before he was supplementing his studies with playing for money—and good money, too. Little by little his fame grew until last year his performance of that Tchaikovsky concerto at Berlin set the whole musical world in a furor. You know the rest—and so does everyone else. Since then his every move has been chronicled in the daily press. Really, I don't know as the boy has bought a pair of shoes that someone hasn't reported it!"

"I wonder how he likes that part of it," mused the girl aloud.

"Not much, I fancy," laughed Preston, a sudden vision coming to him of a small boy peering from behind a picture in his studio and demanding, "Are they gone yet?" "Of course, now he gets fabulous prices for his playing," Preston continued. "For some time he has been really embarrassing me sending money to be spent for his father."

"Sure enough, there was a father—and he's still living, it appears."

"Oh, yes. He has a beautiful room and all possible comforts in a private hospital over near Riverside Drive. The man is greatly changed—but he cannot live much longer, I fear. It was a terrific struggle at first, with disease and his appetite for drink both to fight. He was at a sort of reformatory sanatorium when Marco went away. As I said, it was terrific for a year or two, then gradually he began to improve, so that he could really work a good deal out of doors among the flowers and about the grounds. He developed a real genius for that sort of thing, too, and we thought we'd solved the problem. But last year he began to go back again. Something new set in, and he had to go to the hospital for treatment. Really, I think the only thing that's kept him alive is his love for Marco and his intense interest in the boy's success. The nurse tells me that he treasures every word that he can find about him in the papers, and he is so wild to see him that she fears the result of the meeting."

"The poor man! But joy doesn't often kill, does it? No wonder he's proud of his son. He's not the only one, either, who is 'wild' to see him," smiled Florence as she rose from the table. "Judging from the papers, New York itself is merely killing time until next Tuesday night when he plays. I'm not sure but I'm a little 'wild' myself to meet him," she added merrily. "It all seems so like a wonderful fairy tale."

"It is—a regular 'Aladdin's Lamp' tale," retorted Preston, rising also. "Only the trouble is, now that I have rubbed the lamp, I'm afraid of the genius I've evoked. Anyway, there's nothing to do but to go to the boat tomorrow and meet this Signor Marco Covino."

"Oh, but he isn't 'Signor' at all," laughed Florence, "except when he has to be—in print, you know. Mrs. Fernald told me that he preferred to be 'Marco' to his friends, and 'Mister Covino' instead of 'Signor.' She says he's very fond of America and of everything American."

"Good!" cried Preston heartily, as he turned and held open the door.

CHAPTER 30

Preston had no difficulty in recognizing the man he had come to meet. In the first place, the press agent of the famous violinist had seen to it that the New York papers were well supplied with his likeness for at least a month before his arrival, and Preston had many times studied the pictured features and noted the changes that eight years of foreign training had wrought. If he had needed anything else, he might have found it in the buzz of excited voices around him when Covino appeared, and in the adoring, "There he is—I saw him in Paris last year!" from a very pretty girl who stood close by.

As for Preston—Marco needed no enterprising press agent nor admiring matinee girls to help him in the recognition. Preston at twenty-nine had the same clear, gray eyes, and the same artistic little point to his silky, bronze beard that had distinguished him eight years before; and in the shortest possible time, the two men were clasping hands and gazing eagerly into each other's faces.

Just what they said first neither one could have told afterward; Preston knew only that he had not said half of what he wanted to say when he became unpleasantly aware that he had come to meet, not the unknown boy he had sent away, but the famous artist, to welcome the man for whom half of New York seemed to be waiting in the shape of impatient managers, newspaper men, delegations of all sorts and sizes, and a curious public.

"I'll be out this evening after dinner, if I may," laughed Marco, as he reluctantly turned from Preston's side. "I shan't ask you to come to me, for I want to get away from—this," he finished under his breath. And again Preston had a vision of a small boy peering from behind the picture in his studio and demanding, "Are they gone yet?"

At home Preston was met by the eagerly questioning eyes of Florence.

"Well?" she cried.

"Yes, it is 'well,' I think," smiled the man, "and very well, too. He's all right—not spoiled a bit. He's as simple as the boy I used to know, and as fine as the man I hoped he'd be. He's coming out this evening, and you can see for yourself."

"Tonight? Oh, what a shame! It's Polly's wedding, you know, and I have to be bridesmaid. I shan't see him."

"Never mind, Puss. Mother gives a dinner for him next Wednesday evening, and you'll see him then," laughed Preston. "He's really coming, too, you understand; and I suppose that is something of a triumph. Anyhow, Mother so impressed me with the grave importance of getting his immediate consent before anybody else got a chance to gobble him up that I am not sure I didn't greet him with: 'How do you do, sir? Will you please dine with us next Wednesday night?'"

"Then I suppose I shall have to be content with that," sighed Florence. "And it's only Thursday now. Only think—almost a week to wait! How shall I endure it?" she finished mischievously.

"Oh, but he plays Tuesday night, remember? You'll see him then."

"So I shall! I forgot that," laughed the girl, as she turned away.

Neither Mrs. Preston nor Florence appeared when Marco called at eight o'clock, and only Howard Preston received the young man in the library; but to Marco, at least, there seemed to be nothing lacking in the evening's enjoyment. For three long hours, the two men sat before the dancing flames in the fireplace and talked. And when those three hours had passed, Preston knew the history of those eight years of study and struggle and success. He knew something of the boy's temptations and triumphs, both musically and morally, and he knew something of what this homecoming meant to the youth who had tried so hard to "make good." But he did not know—from Marco—anything about the adoring public that had cast itself at the young violinist's feet.

"And your father—you have seen him?" Preston asked, as his visitor arose to go.

A shadow crossed the younger man's face.

"Yes. He was happy and comfortable—and so changed; but I had hoped to find him better. Poor Dad!" he murmured, and after a pause, "He had every New York paper spread out on his bed when I got there, with my picture staring up at him from each one. After all, it makes him happy, and I'm glad he's pleased. It almost reconciles me to all this—" he shrugged his shoulders with a smile as a finish to his sentence.

CHAPTER 31

On Tuesday evening, the widely heralded young violinist, Signor Marco Covino, made his bow to a brilliant, fashionable, and critical New York audience that meant to decide for itself whether this slender, clean-shaven, dark-eyed young man was really the wonder he was reported to be.

Perhaps half the audience knew that the man had played his violin as a boy on their own city streets. A very much smaller portion had a vivid recollection of a youth who played under the most dramatic circumstances at Mrs. Preston's musicale eight years before. But where there had been moonlight and romance, there was now the pitiless glare of electric lights and critical practicality. A still smaller portion of the audience had heard him more recently in Paris, London, or Berlin. These last fortunate individuals sat back in their chairs with an air of calm superiority—they knew what the verdict would be.

One charmingly pretty girl in pale blue, with a crown of golden hair, watched the violinist with curious absorption from the moment of his first appearance. Her eyes grew dark, as with a haunting memory that refused to materialize into words. That it was not all the music which was causing her close interest was evidenced later, when, during a pause in the program, she leaned forward in her chair and said: "Mother, where have I seen that man before? Didn't we see him once somewhere when we were in Europe a year ago?"

"Nonsense, Florence," laughed the lady. "Of course we didn't! We tried to, once, but I was ill, and we couldn't go to the concert. Don't you remember? At all events, we didn't see him. One doesn't meet

Signor Covino, and then forget it."

"But I have seen him; I know I've seen him."

"You've seen his picture, my dear, like all the rest of us, at every turn. That is all. Or perhaps you did see him when he used to come to the house, years ago."

"No, I never saw him then," returned the girl, decidedly. "I know that, for I took special pains not to see him. Jealousy—of my big brother," she explained, coloring slightly as she answered the surprised look in the other's eyes. "But I have seen this man somewhere. I—" The music interrupted her words, and she leaned back in her chair, the puzzled look still deep in her eyes.

New York went wild the next morning, as only New York can—sometimes. The press, with one accord, hailed the violinist as one of the greatest virtuosos of the day; and the critics vied with each other in lauding his purity of intonation, his beauty of tone, his keen rhythmic feeling, and his astounding mastery of technical difficulties. Every selection that he had played—with one exception—was something already well known to lovers of the violin; but the critics declared that each one was like a new creation, so rare was his skill of interpretation, so marvelously did he throw into each one the dignity, fire, and charm of his own individuality. The one novelty among his selections was a composition of his own, recently finished; and upon this the critics were no less lavish in bestowing their praise, hailing him, indeed, as a great artist in composition as well as in interpretation.

As to the verdict of the feminine world of fashion—the young violinist's rooms were heavy with the scent of innumerable floral offerings; and his wastebasket overflowed with perfumed notes and invitations to countless social functions—the most of which he refused. To Mrs. Preston's, on Wednesday evening, however, he went.

Mrs. Preston welcomed him cordially and with evident appreciation of the honor of his presence. In the background, her son smiled a little—he was thinking of the expression of consternation that the first visit of this young man had brought into his mother's face eight years before.

There was to be a dinner, followed by the musicale. So far as was possible, Mrs. Preston had invited to the latter the same guests that had attended her now famous musicale eight years before. She had achieved one other dramatic victory, too: Marco was to play—and had agreed to play in the alcove, with the music-room darkened. Even nature had lent her aid and had obligingly provided a great full moon.

To be sure, Marco himself had strongly objected to this arrangement. He preferred electric lights and conventionality; but at Mrs. Preston's evident disappointment, he seemed disturbed. Then he chuckled suddenly, and said, with his old boyish twang:

"Sure, Mis' Preston, I'll do it for you. Mr. Preston here's been mighty good to me, and I'd do that and more for him and you!"

For an instant Mrs. Preston stared; then she laughed softly and clapped her hands.

"Thank you. You're splendid! And I believe you could act as well as play, you gifted creature," she added over her shoulder, as she hurried away.

Among Mrs. Preston's guests, there was one, at least, who had not been present eight years before. She was a charming girl in white, with turquoises at her throat and in her hair. Eight years before she had been in bed downstairs, blinking sleepily. Tonight she was very much awake, and her eyes shone like stars when young Covino was presented to her. He started a little as she gave him her hand and smiled frankly into his eyes.

"I'm glad to meet you, Mr. Covino," she said, cordially, "and know the man with whom I shared my big brother eight years ago."

"Thank you—then I did see you long ago!" he exclaimed. "That explains it."

"Oh, but you didn't see me," smiled the girl. "As I remember, I kept very carefully out of your way. I was inclined to be jealous, I'm afraid, of my brother's affection. I didn't relish sharing it."

"But, surely, I—" The announcement of dinner cut short his words. After that he could only watch her covertly from across the table, where he sat at Mrs. Preston's side. It was not, indeed, until after coffee was served and the men had deserted their cigars, that he found an opportunity to speak to her again. Then, abruptly, he went straight to the point.

"Isn't there a people somewhere, Miss Preston, who believe we meet sometimes a man or a woman whom we have known, perhaps, in another life, centuries before? Isn't there a poem that begins, 'When you were an Egyptian princess, and I was a—"some kind of a slave"?'"

Covino's voice was light, but his eyes were grave and carried a curious intentness in their depths.

Miss Preston started and threw a hurried glance into his face. "Really," she laughed, in some embarrassment, "I'm not sure that my stock of poetry isn't somewhat limited. Still, it seems to me I have heard something of the kind—once."

"But—were you the Egyptian princess?" he questioned softly. For a moment he held her gaze unswervingly. She was looking at him, half fascinated, half terrified. Then he changed his position and lifted his head with a quizzical smile. "I have met you somewhere. I wonder where it was!"

The girl laughed in relief, as if some tension had snapped. "Now that you've left the cobwebby past and brought matters down to everyday light," she rejoined, brightly, "I don't mind owning up that I feel as if I had met you somewhere."

"Good! Suppose we compare notes, then. Let us begin with eight years ago, as long as you're so positive that you were unkind enough to keep yourself quite out of my sight before that."

"We will," agreed the girl, promptly. "I've been abroad twice since then, and, of course, somewhere we must have met over there, for you certainly haven't been back here. I'll begin with my first trip, and I'll tell you where I went and when; then we can trace this fugitive impression that we've met each other to its lair." And she launched into a minute description of her travels.

The "fugitive impression," however, refused to be captured, and neither Covino nor Miss Preston was any nearer the solution of the puzzle.

Marco picked up his violin and played a curious melody from a piece of music that lay before him—a weird little phrase that made him stop abruptly.

"Why, how odd!" he murmured. "That is almost exactly like it."

"Like what?"

"A little tune that I used to play years ago."

"Perhaps it's the same," suggested the girl. "It sounded almost familiar to me, too. I think I have heard it somewhere."

"Oh, but you couldn't have heard it," objected Marco, "because it's one of my own that I fashioned myself long ago, when a boy. It was never published. Besides, this one is quite new and, of course, it isn't the same. It only reminded me of a part of it."

"Yours? One of your own? Play it. Did I ever hear it?"

"I think not. I haven't played it much lately, except when alone. It's a sad little thing and has only sorrowful memories for me. I had such great hopes of what would some time come from it—and it failed me. However, you shall hear it." He raised his violin to position and softly drew the bow across the strings in the first strains of "Lost on the Ocean Wave."

Before the piece was ended, Florence was on her feet, her eyes startled and questioning. When it was finished, she clapped her hands lightly.

"I have heard it! That was the piece—not this," she cried, tapping the new music on the rack before her.

"But, Florence, how could you? That is my piece!"

"I don't know, but I did hear it. It was when—" she paused, and half closed her eyes. In the dim past of her memory she was groping for a clue that would help her. "It was—there was a picture, all sky and sea, and—and one little boat—all—alone," she finished dreamily, just above her breath.

The color fled from Marco's face. Even his lips were bloodless.

"I don't know. I think—it was in a book—a little book with green covers, and the picture was—was—'Lost on the Ocean Wave.' Now I have it!" she exulted, turning to him in gleeful triumph. The next instant she stepped back. "Marco—why, Marco!" she cried.

Marco laid down his violin and placed the bow carefully at its side. Then he turned back to the girl and sat down near her. Outwardly he was calm, but his voice shook when he spoke.

"Florence, try to remember; tell me all that you can of yourself before you came here—to live."

She shook her head, and her eyes grew thoughtful. "There isn't much that I can tell. I was very small, not more than seven or eight, and Mrs. Preston has never let me talk of those days. All she told me was that I was the daughter of her dearest friend, who was dead. She said that for some years after I was born she didn't know where I was; then they found me in a gypsy camp—"

"Then it is true—it is true!" cried Marco

"What is true? What do you mean?" demanded the girl, her voice sharp with excitement. Then something sent her thoughts back to the cause of his first cry, and she caught at that to find a possible explanation.

"That little melody—I remember now," she went on, hurriedly. "It was there that I heard it—in the gypsy camp. There was a boy—my brother—" she stopped suddenly. Her face grew white. With a sharp cry, she sprang to her feet and threw her arms around the man.

"Marco! You are my Marco!"

CHAPTER 32

In the sick-room, John Covino sat propped up in bed with several pillows at his back. His dark hair had turned almost white at the temples, and his cheeks were sunken pitifully. But his eyes were bright and told of a clear brain behind them. As his son entered the room, he smiled and held out his hand.

"Marco!" he cried, rapturously.

For some minutes the two men talked common-place nothings. Marco was hesitating to broach any deeper subject; then he could wait no longer.

"Father, I've some news for you," he began, a little tremulously. "You know long ago, Father, you had a daughter—a little Florence, my sister." Marco was speaking hurriedly now. He had thought to lead up to this thing more gradually, but the strain was becoming unbearable, and his dry lips were almost refusing to articulate the words. "Well, this older Florence, that I've recently met, is Mrs. Preston's adopted daughter, and we discovered yesterday that she and the little Florence of long ago are the same, Father. Your little daughter has come back to you a beautiful young woman. She wants to come to see you," finished Marco, turning to his father, who had closed his eyes.

Marco watched in silence. Then his father opened his eyes and studied Marco's face.

"Marco," he began, quietly, "You do not seem overjoyed at this news."

"Oh, I am! I just—Well, I searched for Flossie for so many years, and I am just so surprised to find her as a—as a woman—a very beautiful woman. It feels a little strange."

"Marco, listen to me carefully. I have some important things to tell you. I don't want you to think I don't realize what you have done for me all these years. I don't want you to think I'm ungrateful. There have been times when I've blamed myself bitterly, when I've known that I've done wrong from the very beginning. But I think now—now—I can set things straight. I'll have to go back—way back, so you'll understand, but it won't take long.

"I was nothing but a boy when my mother died. I don't remember much about my home except that it had wide, green meadows where my brother and I played all day and a big stone house where we slept all night. After that something happened. We lost our money, I suppose. Anyhow, we drifted about from place to place, and then one day, Father took both us boys and came to America. Even now I can remember the misery of those first few years. My father had been gently born. He was not used to hardship and poverty, and here he found both. Then, one day, when we boys were twenty or thereabouts, a man came along and hired all three of us to go down by the Mississippi River to grow cotton. It sounded good to us. We'd have the sky and the earth and the soft air of the Southland, and we liked those better than we did the dirty, noisy streets where we were.

"We went, but we hadn't been there a week before we saw our mistake. We had the sky, but we had the hot sun too, and we had the earth, but that was full of swamps and still lakes with a green slime on top. The air was there, too, but it swarmed with mosquitoes. And then there was the work. That was bad enough, but it wasn't nothing to the treatment we got. The boss was used to drivin' slaves—and he drove us like slaves, and with slaves, too, just 'cause our hair and eyes and skin was dark.

"Until then Father had kept up something of what he had been. He'd sent us to school when he could and had taught us himself when he couldn't. But he gave up now. He caught the fever, and in three weeks after we got there he was dead.

"Naturally, we boys didn't stay long then. Already lots of them that had gone down there with us had got away, and we wasn't long in following. Then come the gypsies. We run across them one night after we'd been tramping the woods all day, tired and hungry. They took us in, and we just stayed, and sort of drifted along with them. It was easy, and we liked it. We could already sing, and pretty soon we'd picked up the banjo and guitar. After that we didn't have any trouble but what we could earn a penny or two when we liked. Then come your mother."

The man paused and closed his eyes. His son drew a deep breath. "The little mumsey!" he cried softly. The other did not seem to hear, and in a moment he had resumed his story.

"I wish you could have seen her as I did," he said, dreamily. "She was so pretty and so young—less than eighteen. She was the daughter of a famous violinist. You'll find his name and all about him in some papers I've got, but never mind that now. They had a country house near where we had set up camp one summer. There were a lot of gay young folks there, and they got to running down to our tents pretty often to have their fortunes told, and for a lark generally. We went there too, and sang and played for them at their garden parties—especially me and my brother.

"From the very first, your mother and I took to each other, and I was there a lot with my guitar. It wasn't long, of course, before we had fallen in love and owned it up to each other. It was my fault, of course. I knew perfectly well I was no fit mate for her, but I was young and I didn't care—or rather, I cared too much. Still, it's a question whether anything would have come of it if the old violinist hadn't set his heart on her marrying another man, and an old one at that. She bolted then, and flew to me, before she had even had time to think of the consequences. We broke camp then, and she went with us—my wife."

Again the man paused and moistened his lips. His face had grown gray with pain. For some time, he had been speaking brokenly and with evident constraint, but at a word from his son that he should rest, he shook his head decidedly.

"No, I'm going to tell it—though it isn't easy—the part that comes now. I've thought sometimes I wouldn't tell, but you've been square by me, and I'm ashamed not to be square by you. You've made me see things, too—your religion counts for something. Your mother's did, too. And that's what makes it so hard—now. Looking back at it, I don't see how I did it, anyway. After all, it was always drink that was at the bottom of it. Naturally—the life I'd led—my habits weren't the best. I realized, too, that the way I was living was no place for—her. And I was ashamed. We quarreled sometimes, though it was never her fault. She was always good to me.

"When you were three years old, my brother died. I left your mother then, with the gypsies and tried to get good, steady work. I promised to go back and get her when I'd found it. But I wasn't used to work, and I didn't take to it very well. Everything seemed to be against me, too, and I went from bad to worse. Every little while I'd make a new start, but drink—or something—would pull me down again.

"I kept track of the gypsies, and once in a while I'd go to see your mother, but I don't think by that time my visits did her or anyone else much good. I tried to have her go back to her people. But she was proud and wouldn't go. Her father had cast her off, anyhow, and had sent word that he never wanted to see her again. So, naturally, she didn't want him to know how—how bad things had turned out.

Besides, she still declared that she believed some time I'd—make good.

"I went away then and tried harder than ever, but it was no use. After that I only came back to the gypsies on the sly. I saw you often, though you didn't know me, but I kept out of the way of your mother. I didn't know she was dead until long afterwards, and I found you gone, too. That was the night I got crazy drunk and thought I had killed—a man. Then is when I skipped that part of the country and changed my name. The man didn't die, and I came back, but I kept the name. After that I saw you—you know the rest. I'd kept the name then so long, I had to change yours."

"Then I am really—Marco Bonelli?"

"Yes, but there is more. You were two years old when, one day, a train went through a trestle near our camp. It was a fearful sight, but your mother never flinched. She went right into the thick of it and worked without a thought of herself. In one dead woman's arms she found a little girl baby, about eight or ten months old. No one claimed it, and she took it home to the tent and took care of it. She thought surely someone would come for it some time, but no one did, and at last she got to look upon it as her own. But it wasn't. It was—"

"Florence!" interrupted Marco with a choking cry.

"Yes, Florence—Flossie."

"But—I don't understand. Mrs. Preston knew her mother. She says Florence was the daughter of her dearest friend. How could that be?"

"I can explain that, too," murmured the sick man. With a pang Marco noticed how wearily he spoke. "I saw old Uncle Jake of the gypsy camp long afterwards, and he told me Flossie was gone. He said a man came for her. The man had said that his wife had been a very dear friend of Flossie's mother and that she had supposed the whole family was killed in the accident. Long afterwards, she had run across a woman who had been in the wreck and who told her all about the baby that the gypsy woman had taken from the dead woman's arms. From the description she recognized her friend; and ever since then she had been tracing that baby, until at last she had found her—Flossie. So you see—it's all—straight, to the last," finished the man faintly.

* * *

After Marco left his father, he almost ran into a crippled little fellow in the hallway.

"I beg your pardon, sir," stammered the boy, confusedly, yet with unmistakable satisfaction. "It's just that I wanted to see you—and I did, too!"

"To see me? What for? What can I do for you, my lad?"

"Nothin', sir. You've done it. We just wanted to see ye—all of us," he finished, and with a flourish of his hands, Marco suddenly became aware that from half a dozen beds and doorways peered as many pairs of eager, boyish eyes. "Ye see, we knew who you were," explained the boy, in answer to the man's mystified gaze, "and so we wanted to see you—as long as we couldn't hear you play."

"Hear me play? Why, of course you can hear me play," retorted Marco, promptly, with sudden inspiration. "I fancy I can arrange a little matter like that!"

Thus it happened that on the very day upon which a certain multi-millionaire was gnawing his mustache with vexation because even his millions could not buy for him the musical toy of the hour which he so coveted, that same musical "toy" was causing a score of little twisted feet and legs to beat time to a rollicking "Money Musk" played as "Money Musk" had seldom been played before.

It occurred to Marco after this that there were other hospitals, besides numberless infirmaries and asylums, where frail humanity was debarred from almost every joy. He wondered if perhaps he had not some joy to give them, through his violin, and he decided to find out. He found out—and so did his manager.

The manager wept and tore his hair, figuratively. He declared that it was unheard of, preposterous, and quixotic, besides being suicidal to the great violinist's art, career, and pocketbook. He said many other things, too; but the violinist only smiled inscrutably—and looked up another hospital. After all, the manager was little more than a figurehead, as the contract between them had been drawn by Marco himself, with an eye to his own repugnance to having his actions controlled. The three concerts at which the violinist was to play before the season ended—two in Boston and one in New York—would soon be over; and after that, the manager would doubtless shake the dust of the city off his feet and go back to his beloved Paris, leaving Marco alone for his summer vacation. Marco knew this and was accordingly content.

In Gaylordville, at about this time, there was another surprise. It centered in the little house where the Widow Martin was still trying to get the tin coffee pot full enough of money to take her family back to the New Hampshire hills.

Grandpa Joe was long since dead, and Susie had married and gone away. She had come back, though, in widow's weeds, in less than two years; and the Widow Martin now longed, more intensely than ever, for the New Hampshire hills, for the sake of Baby Sue, Susie's little girl. Of the boys, Johnny was still there, thin-faced, stoop-shouldered, and old before his time; but Benny had gone. Benny went down into the mine one day—and did not come back. The Widow Martin thought of this sometimes when she watched her last-born start for his work in the morning. At such times she was apt to take down the tin coffee pot and count its wealth—she would like the New Hampshire hills for Johnny, too. The doctor said that disease would kill him, if the mines themselves did not, before long.

It was into this household that the surprise came. The surprise took the shape of a wonderful being who looked like a man—but who was in reality an angel, according to all the stories that the Martins told afterward.

This man (or angel) appeared one day in their midst and calmly announced that he long ago owed them eight dollars and forty cents, and that this eight dollars and forty cents had been accumulating interest all these years. Interest, he said, was a marvelous thing; it grew wonderfully, but he had come now prepared to pay. And he placed upon the table the eight dollars and forty cents, and with it such a stupendous sum of money that the entire Martin family could do nothing the whole evening but hover over it and count it at regular intervals, to make sure that they had not, after all, been mistaken.

In the morning they gathered themselves together, picked up their few belongings, and as soon as possible started for the New Hampshire hills. But even after they had reached them, they looked into each other's faces and wondered how it had all happened.

The Martins, however, were not the only ones that had strange visitors during the first few weeks after Marco Covino arrived in New York. A little hunchback newsman, who had a tiny store near a crowded Third Avenue corner, found himself confronted one day by a slender, smooth-shaven young fellow, dark-haired and dark-eyed.

"Well, well," cried the stranger, holding out a cordial hand, "I've had the chase of my life to locate you—but I've found you at last. How are you?"

Behind the counter the little man's eyes narrowed shrewdly. "Get out of here! I've seen that game tried once too often, stranger, to be fooled at my time of life—only they don't generally take a chap like me."

"Why, Jimmy, don't you know me?"

"Sure, no—Mike," grinned the hunchback. "Come! Go on now, and leave an honest man to his work."

"But you see I know your name, Jimmy."

"So does half the avenue, to say nothin' of the streets what crosses it."

The stranger laughed. "I thought my job was done when I'd found you, Jimmy, but it seems it's just begun. How's the mother, and the baby-what-was, ten or twelve years ago? Been to Mont-Lawn lately?"

The hunchback stared; then he laid both elbows on the counter with slow deliberation. "Say, who be you, anyhow?" he demanded.

"If I had my fiddle here I might play you a little tune and see if you couldn't guess," retorted the man with a smile.

A dawning comprehension sent a gleam of joyful amazement into the hunchback's eyes. "Marco! Say, now, you aren't Marco!"

"Why, I thought I was, but—" his words were cut short. With a monkey-like spring, the little man had leaped upon the counter and caught hold of both his hands.

"Why, sure you're Marco! And a sight for sore eyes you are, too! and so you've struck New York again! Well, you're looking fine, boy! And to think I didn't know ye! Say, why didn't you bring your fiddle and play us a tune? It would-a been a good joke. Maybe you don't play though now, eh?"

"Oh, yes, I play," rejoined Marco, quietly. "By the way, I brought you in a couple of concert tickets for tomorrow night. You see, I remembered you liked music, and I thought you might like to go to this," he concluded, handing out two little oblong slips of thin pasteboard which—had Jimmy but known it—might have been at that moment worth their weight in gold to certain disappointed, would-be ticket buyers over on the avenue, who had just been told that the house was "all sold out a week ago."

"Thank you," murmured Jimmy, somewhat doubtfully receiving the oblong slips. "Course, I don't get away much, though I've got a man to help me," he added, with a jerk of his thumb toward a red-headed boy who was selling magazines and papers at the other counter. "But Katy—she's the baby-what-was, you know; she's a big girl now—she likes music somethin' awful, and I'll take her. Thank ye; I'll go."

"I don't think you'll be sorry if you do," smiled the man. Then he asked, with apparent casualty, "How is it?—business pretty good?"

A quick cloud shadowed the hunchback's face.

"Yes, and it would be better if I had money and room to branch out. I been savin', but I can't get much ahead. You see, there's Mother—she isn't well; and Katy's got to have some schoolin'. I'd hoped to do somethin' handsome by Katy, and make a lady of her, but I don't know as I can get to it 'fore she gets old and gray-headed. But tell me about yourself. Where you been?"

Marco laughed. "Oh, that will keep until another time," he parried as he turned away. "I shall have to go now, but you'll see me again soon. Don't forget the concert tomorrow night, you know."

"I won't. Katy won't let me, anyhow, if she once gets her eyes on them tickets!"

As it happened, Katy got her eyes on the tickets very soon,

for she came into the store on an errand, and after that there was certainly little chance of Jimmy's forgetting the concert.

There were those in the great audience, assembled to hear the famous young violinist play in his second concert the next night, who wondered just how it happened that two of the best seats in the front row of the first balcony were occupied by an insignificant hunchback and a pale-faced, poorly-dressed little girl. The couple were neat and respectable-looking, to be sure; but they certainly did seem a little out of place in the richly-dressed throng that filled every seat and crowded every available bit of standing-room.

The hunchback himself acted nervous, and fingered his program restlessly, gazing at it with curious eyes. Then suddenly he gave a start.

"Say, Katy," he whispered hoarsely, "there's a chap what's put down here on this 'ere paper as one of the performers, and his name is 'Signor Marco Covino.' Now, our Marco's name is Covino—though I'd 'most forgot it till now. You don't s'pose—but then, it couldn't be! Our Marco wouldn't be playin' here 'fore all this swell crowd."

"Course not," murmured Katy, her awestruck eyes devouring the glitter and sparkle afloat about her.

"Course not," echoed the man, falling back in his seat. But that he was not quite convinced was shown a moment later when he hesitatingly nudged the arm of his neighbor on the other side—a very fleshy woman resplendent in diamonds.

"I beg pardon, ma'am," he began humbly, "but I heard you talkin' about this 'ere Marco Covino,"—tapping his program—"and I just wanted to ask you, is he a slim, quiet-spoken chap in a gray suit, with—"

"Signor Covino is one of the greatest violinists living," coldly interrupted she of the diamonds. "Surely, anyone who has come to hear him play should know that," she said as she turned severely back to her program.

"Yes'm. Thank you. I knew, course, it wasn't the same one," murmured the hunchback apologetically, as he subsided in some confusion.

***

In the newspapers the next morning, there were glowing accounts of the great ovation given to the famous violinist upon his appearance. In at least one of the accounts this incident was mentioned:

"The applause in the first balcony was led by a curious little hunchback who was dancing up and down in his seat and cheering like mad. Those who were nearest to him said that no sooner had the violinist stepped into view than this little hunchback gave one startled look, then sprang to his feet, yelling, 'Marco—Marco—it is Marco!' By that time, the whole house was wildly cheering, the wildest of all still being the excited little hunchback in the balcony seat."

CHAPTER 33

Jimmy's friends will tell you that about this time Jimmy had a "streak of luck." Certain it is that he began almost at once to have "money and room to branch out," as he had said that he wished he did have. Luxuries too crept into the home for the invalid mother, and a stout woman came to relieve Katy of care and to enable her to go to school more regularly.

Jimmy could have told you—but he would not, because he had promised not to tell—that Marco Covino was at the bottom of it all. Not that he, Jimmy, was accepting charity—certainly not. But Covino said he already owed the Nolans a great deal for past kindnesses, and nothing that he could ever do would repay them. As for the rest—he was merely making an investment on his own account and helping Jimmy to take advantage of some exceptionally good business opportunities that had just come up.

Early in June, Marco left the city, in acceptance of Mrs. Preston's invitation to come down to their country place on Long Island.

Marco had already seen a good deal of the Prestons, and he looked forward to this visit with no little eagerness. He told himself that it was because he would once more be out under a wide blue sky, with the green out-of-doors all about him; but he knew perfectly well that this was not the only reason for his anticipated enjoyment: the companions with whom he would share this wide blue sky and green out-of-doors had something to do with it.

Marco liked the Prestons. He was thinking of them now as he was being swiftly borne toward their house. Howard Preston he considered his best friend. Mrs. Preston he considered a charming woman and a delightful hostess. Florence he considered—and here he stopped abruptly: it had come to him just how much he was considering this young woman with the peculiarly haunting eyes and the soft halo of gold.

Then, too, their tastes were congenial. She played the piano with no little skill and had tried many of his accompaniments. He enjoyed playing with her very much. She delighted, too, in outdoor life, and they had many plans for tennis, golf, boating, and picnicking, to say nothing of riding and driving. Certainly he had reason to anticipate his coming play-day very joyfully.

Upon his arrival at the Prestons', Marco found a large house-party for the weekend; but by Tuesday, nearly all had gone back to the city, leaving only a very charming girl with a piquant face and a merry laugh—Madge Dana.

Marco liked Miss Dana at once. He said she "fitted in" just right, but it is doubtful if he realized that the reason she did "fit in" (so far as he was concerned) was because she made an ever-present fourth in their merrymakings, thus leaving Florence more exclusively to himself. To Marco, therefore, it was a most delightful arrangement, and the month of June passed all too soon.

On the first day of July, Marco announced that he must go back to the city for a few days.

"Nonsense!" remonstrated Mrs. Preston. "As if there could be anything that needed your attention in that hot, stuffy city in July!"

"But there is."

Mrs. Preston frowned. Then her eyes grew anxious.

"Now, my dear boy, there's no one, surely, who admires all your numerous good deeds which are so constantly cropping up, more than I do. But I think you owe something to yourself as well as to all those hospitals and asylums and countless ragamuffins that you are so fond of. Why, Florence," she added, turning to the girl at her side, "do you know? I heard the other day that this Don Quixote of ours actually spent whole days tramping the worst streets of New York in search of a little hunchback boy whom he used to know years ago!"

Marco made a gesture of annoyance.

"I thought I had kept that a secret, at least," he muttered.

"So it was true, then!"

This time, in spite of his vexation, the man laughed outright. "If that is the way I let things out, I ought not to wonder that I can't keep things, surely!" he exclaimed, in obvious disgust with himself.

At that moment Mrs. Preston was called from the room, and only the girl was left to question him.

"I wish you'd tell me about it—the little hunchback," she entreated, her eyes luminous with feeling.

Marco shook his head. "It was nothing—really."

"But is it for him that you go now?"

"No, oh, no."

"It isn't your father, for you said yesterday he was doing well; besides, you ran in to see him only last week."

"No, it isn't Father, though I shall go out to see him, of course. They don't like to have me come too often, anyhow, you know—it excites him so much to see me. The nurse says letters are better. There's something curious about it. In spite of his love for me, it seems to work him all up to see me, sometimes."

"And still you must go to the city and leave us," she murmured.

"And still I must go to the city and leave—you."

At the last word, she colored a little; he had contrived to make it particularly personal.

"But you're coming back," she reminded him, hurriedly.

"If I may, soon after the Fourth, perhaps."

"Why, of course you are coming back! You promised us all of June and July."

"You mean, Mrs. Preston promised me all of June and July," he corrected, and again the girl colored—much to her vexation—at the personal touch he had given his answer.

"We shall miss you—all of us," she murmured, with some precipitation. "Madge was saying only this morning what a pleasant party we made."

"You have been very good to me. You have made me like one of the family," returned the man gratefully.

"And you are one of the family," declared Mrs. Preston, coming back into the room at that moment. And she did not notice that for some time afterward Florence did not speak.

It was on the second of the month that the Prestons' distinguished guest went to New York, and for some days nothing was heard from him except a short note addressed to Howard Preston. Then, on the sixth came a letter to Florence from a school friend—a letter which speedily sent Florence, with flushed cheeks and shining eyes, into Mrs. Preston's room.

"Mother," she cried, tremulously, "just listen to this. It's from Elizabeth Bennett. You know she's gone as a sort of teacher or caretaker to that children's vacation home, Mont-Lawn. Listen! I'll skip to the part I want you to hear." And she read aloud:

"Do you know, Florence, what that adorable young violinist of yours has been up to now? No, of course you don't, for he's tried to be as secret as the grave about it. As if he could—Covino! Well, he's been up here playing. Only think of it—playing! And to these three hundred kiddies who don't own enough money, probably, the whole bunch of them, to buy a single ticket to one of his concerts!

"Now for the story.

"You may not know, but they make a great deal of the Fourth here, with invited guests from all around, and with usually three or four more or less noted speakers. Yesterday we were having our speeches, as usual, on the lawn, when during a pause a slender, dark-eyed young fellow, who had been strolling about the grounds before the exercises, asked permission to speak to the children. It was granted, of course, and then he began.

"He said that ten or twelve years ago he, too, had been a boy here and that he owed to this place the tenderest reverence, for here he first learned to be 'red, white, and blue.' Naturally such an odd way of putting it made everybody sit up, and we heard then the most wonderful word-painting that I have ever listened to, as he went on to describe what he saw and heard here and how it had affected him. Long before he had finished, and I saw all humanity in one glorious throng marching on to be red, white, and blue, so contagious was his enthusiasm.

"Then, very quietly, after it was all over, he attempted to fade away. But he couldn't do it. Of course, the most of us hadn't the faintest idea who he was, but there were some on the speakers' platform who had a very decided idea, and they called him by name.

"It was all over, then, naturally. He was plainly dismayed to be recognized, but when he found there was no help for it, he made the best of it and behaved like a dear. Someone was bold enough to say something about his playing for us, and he laughingly retorted that if only he had his violin he would. He supposed he was safe, poor man! But he little knew that crowd. In five minutes they had a score of scouts out in all directions with instructions to bring back anything that looked like a fiddle. And they got one, too. It was a wretched instrument, belonging to an old colored man who lives in a hut half a mile from here. I wish you could have seen Covino's face when they proudly displayed their trophy and announced that now he had his violin.

"At first I thought he was going to refuse. (You know artists are fussy about their instruments, and I don't know as I blame them.) But he gave one look around, and I suppose he saw in our faces what this thing was going to mean for us. So with a funny little gesture, he threw up both his hands and shrugged his shoulders, as much as to say, 'Your crime be upon your own heads!' Then he picked up that wretched violin and actually made it talk. Of course, the children were wild, and in no time they were dancing all over the lawn, while the rest of us—well, the rest of us really pinched ourselves to make sure we were awake.

"You are wondering already why you haven't seen it in the papers. There were only two reporters there, and somehow Covino succeeded in swearing them to secrecy. But, of course, it will be out sometime. Somebody who was here will tell—then goodbye to the secret. But wasn't he a dear to do it?"

"And, Mother, wasn't he?" cried Florence fervently, as she dropped the letter into her lap.

"He certainly was, my dear," agreed Mrs. Preston, her gaze rather anxiously bent on the burning cheeks and star-like eyes of the girl in the low chair by the window.

CHAPTER 34

Various matters kept Marco Covino in New York for some days after the Fourth. It was not until the eighth, indeed, that he finally turned his face toward the Prestons' Long Island home.

To Marco, these days had been momentous ones, for during them he had made a discovery—he had fallen in love. He must have fallen in love, he argued, for in no other way could he account for his restlessness at the enforced delay and for his eagerness to return to the companionship of a certain fair-haired girl. As he looked ahead, life seemed very sweet to him if, to share it with him, there was to be this girl, but he shuddered and closed his eyes as he pictured the dreary waste that same life would be to him without her.

Marco was seriously disturbed. Until now, he had not thought of marriage. Nowhere among the admiring throngs of women that he had met, either at home or abroad, had he found one who had stirred his pulse by so much as an extra beat. The case was different now, however; yet, how was he to tell a woman he loved her?

As Marco thought of it, there seemed to be only one way out at present. He would go to Preston, his best friend, for advice. At all events, Marco decided that at least he would not speak to Florence of his love for her until he had made all possible efforts to find out where he stood.

It was a good resolution, and he meant to keep it, but he almost broke it late that afternoon, for Florence met him at the station with her own pony-phaeton, and they had a tête-à-tête drive home in the twilight. The girl's cheeks were flushed, and her eyes glowed with soft fire. The one thing that was uppermost in her mind, however, she did not mention—the letter she had received from her friend at the children's home.

Just what they did speak of, neither could scarcely have told afterward, perhaps. Florence knew only that the sunset was the most beautiful one she had ever seen and that just to be alive to enjoy it was the most wonderful thing in the world. That there was a hidden something somewhere, however, she must have dimly understood, for she refused to meet Covino's eyes as he helped her from the carriage, and she hurried almost at once into the house.

In Preston's den that evening, after the rest of the family had gone to bed, came Marco's opportunity. The two men were smoking together and had been talking of various matters, when Marco attempted to bring the conversation around to the subject that was so near his heart. He had planned a skillful introduction by which he hoped to lead up to the matter naturally, but at the critical point his throat seemed to contract and his head to swim; the next moment he was exasperated to hear himself stammering a banal, "What a beautiful girl your sister is, Preston!" Certainly that was not the sort of beginning he had meant to make, but before he could speak again, he was silenced by a curious something that had come into Preston's face.

"Yes, she is even more than that, my boy," he was saying quietly, "and I'm rather glad you've brought the matter up. It gives me a good chance to tell you something I've wanted for some time to speak of. Florence is not my sister, you know. She is really no relation whatever."

"I know," murmured the younger man, vainly trying to rally his forces for another and a more skillful attack.

Preston hesitated, then went on, a deeper note in his voice, "I am hoping to make her, sometime, even more nearly—a daughter to my mother."

Across the room a man caught his breath sharply and gripped the arms of his chair with tense fingers.

"You mean as—" Even as he spoke, Marco wondered how his lips had found the strength to form the words.

"As my wife, yes," answered Preston.

There was a dead silence. Across the room the rigid fingers still gripped the senseless wood. The face above had grown gray and cold, like ashes after a long-spent fire.

"You are to be—congratulated. I did—not—know," murmured a sternly controlled voice, after a time.

"No, of course you did not," returned Preston, a little sadly. "In fact, that's exactly the trouble—none of us knows. You see, it's not a certainty at all, only a dear hope. I have not yet won Florence's love."

Marco almost sprang to his feet. A fierce gleam of triumphant joy leaped to his eyes and glowed there a devouring flame. The red blood of a mad hope throbbed at his temples and dinned into his ears the wondrous truth: it was not too late; even yet he might win her love; even yet—he would win it! . . . Then, very suddenly, the flame went out, the red blood ebbed, and the world was gray again. Marco's eyes were on the bowed head of the man opposite, the man who was his friend.

"Perhaps not yet, but you will win it," he said gently, and only to himself was the steadiness of his voice a surprise.

"Thank you," Preston said, gratefully, coming out of his revelry. "We'll hope you're a good prophet, my boy," he added, as Marco rose from his chair, preparatory to saying goodnight.

In his own room a little later, Marco faced this thing that had come to him and tried to realize just what it meant. From Preston he had fled as soon as possible. He dared not trust himself much longer to the danger of the man's questioning eyes. The suddenness of the blow had been like the proverbial bolt from the blue, and not yet had he recovered from the first shock of Preston's confession.

Even thus early, however, he was confident that the only thing for him to do was to go away. That one moment when he was tempted to match his powers of persuasion against the still unsuccessful suit of his friend had been enough to show him that. He certainly did not dare to trust himself to the daily strain of seeing another man try to win the love of the girl he had thought to win for himself; and he certainly, also, had no real intention of placing the smallest barrier in the way of that other man's success, particularly when that other man was Howard Preston, to whom he owed so much.

As he looked at it, therefore, it was merely another case of his old boyhood's "red, white, and blue," and this time it was the part of truth and loyalty and bravery to run away—not to stay. There remained then merely the arrangement of details, for go he must and would.

Marco went to bed then—but not to sleep. He lay awake until far into the morning hours, building plans and tearing them down.

CHAPTER 35

Marco Covino was not the only one who did not sleep on the night after his arrival at the Prestons'. In a dainty blue-and-white bedroom in the east wing, a young girl wearily sought a position where sleep might find her; but sleep was not to be coaxed, and after a time the girl got up, threw a light garment over her shoulders, and seated herself at the window, where she might look out upon the starlit night.

She thought the stars might help her; they seemed so cool and far away and impersonal, but they proved to be altogether too far away and impersonal, while her problem was very near and human. Besides, the stars only reminded her of a moonlit, starlit alcove, with a man playing the violin—and that did not help a bit. Then there was the water, lying before her in a great sea of shadows; but its song was the same that it had sung that afternoon, when she had driven along its shore in the twilight—and that did not help, either. Everywhere she turned, something reminded her of a pair of dark eyes that carried always an eager question in their depths— and this was the least help of all. It was worse than that, indeed, for one of her troubles was the fact that this same pair of dark eyes so constantly looked out at her from the most familiar, everyday surroundings.

Another trouble was Howard. She had decided long ago that the love he asked for was a most natural arrangement and one which was much to be desired as well. She even thought she had planted the seeds, and for some time now she had been confidently looking for her love for him to grow. But it had not grown. On the contrary, a very different plant had come up—a shy, tremulous thing that hid from the light of day and seemed to be rooted in nothing more substantial than a thought, a hand pressure, or the glance of a dark eye. For this alien flower she had planted no seed. It had come up unbidden; while the other—she had even watered that with her tears, yet it had refused to grow.

It was all very pitiful, very much to be deplored, and she could not understand it in the least. With a long sigh, she finally rose and crept back to bed, little the wiser or the happier for her reflection.

Morning brought a subtle change to the atmosphere of the Preston house-party. Florence being the most sensitive, perhaps, noticed it first. It was a curious thing, elusive, and scarcely definable. For some time after she had discovered it, she could not put her finger upon it and say, "Lo, here," or "Lo, there." She knew only that it was present, somewhere. Then, unexpectedly, on the second day she found it—young Covino was constrained, ill at ease; he had entirely lost his friendly air of comradeship, and—she was sure now of this—he unmistakably avoided her.

She told herself that she was glad and that it made an easy way out of her difficulties; for, of course, with nothing to feed upon, that alien flower in the garden of her heart could not grow. She found out very speedily, however, that she was mistaken; for it was upon just this sort of thing that the flower thrived—disgracefully.

On the fourth day, Marco Covino went to New York—to see his father, he said; and three days later came the letter to Mrs. Preston which proved to be something in the nature of a bombshell in its unexpectedness. Mrs. Preston read the letter at the breakfast table; then she gave an exclamation of disappointment.

"Children, what do you suppose is the matter? Mr. Covino is not coming back," she cried.

"Not coming back!" exclaimed her son.

"No. He writes a very pretty letter, and thanks us heartily for all our kindness, but he says that various matters have conspired to prevent his finishing his visit here, as he had at first hoped that he might."

"Oh, what a shame!" regretted Madge Dana. "And he was so delightful!"

"But what is it? What is the matter?" demanded Preston.

Mrs. Preston shook her head.

"I don't know. He says it will be his loss and that he's very sorry. He asks that what he didn't take with him be sent to his hotel at any time that's convenient."

"But it's so odd—it isn't like him a bit," argued Preston.

"And so unexpected," murmured Miss Dana.

"And so very disappointing all around," finished Mrs. Preston, as she tucked the letter into its envelope. And she alone noticed that of all that group at the table, Florence had been the only one to make no comment. It was Mrs. Preston, too, who noted that Florence ate but little breakfast and soon asked to be excused.

CHAPTER 36

In talking of it afterward, Florence and Marco agreed that if it had not happened then, it would have happened at some time not much later. It was one of the kind of things that happen just because they must happen—because the natural trend of two lives leads undeviatingly toward just that crisis.

It was in November and at the first concert that Signor Covino was giving that season—a concert which Florence attended.

The concert was half over when the usher discovered the whiff of smoke curling up from the rear of the first balcony. A woman saw it then and screamed. On the stage Covino was playing with an orchestra forty strong at his back. Covino, too, saw the curl of smoke—but he did not stop playing.

There was more commotion now. Another woman had seen the smoke and had screamed. All over the house men and women had risen by twos and threes, and some were crowding out into the aisles.

From the wings a frenzied voice called to the players, "For goodness sake, don't stop! Play—play—keep them cool!"

And they did play, steadily, splendidly, though by this time half the vast audience was on its feet, and the whiff of smoke had become little darting flames.

Long minutes later, Covino came face to face with a girl who was plunging back through the smoke-filled corridor.

"Florence!"

"Marco!"

And to neither of them did it seem strange that he took her in his arms and kissed her. As it chanced, they were alone in the veil of smoke, but it would have been the same had they met in Broadway at that illuminating moment. Face to face in that moment of peril, they looked into each other's eyes and saw only the supreme truth of their love.

"But, dearest, how came you alone—here?" Even as he spoke, the man had turned her about and was guiding her through the stifling passageway.

"I don't know. I was with the Eatons, and I think—I lost them, some way. I looked back and saw you still playing, and I—I had to come back, that's all. I thought I could reach you this way. There were not many in this corridor, and—I ran."

For answer he pressed her arm tenderly. To neither of them yet had it occurred that there was anything strange in this sudden intimacy. The realization came soon—very soon. One more turn brought them to a wider corridor, and through this they quickly reached one of the exits to the street.

Already the frenzy of terror was subsiding. Everywhere officers and ushers were soothing, directing, and marshaling the throngs into something like order, and their coolness was contagious. It was plain that all danger of a panic was over. Once on the street, Marco forced a way through the surging crowd and was so fortunate as to find almost immediately a carriage to take them home. Then once more he turned and faced her—the realization had come.

Her eyes were still soft and luminous, but to her pale cheeks had come a rosy flush. She, too, had suddenly realized that they were back in the everyday world—that their souls had not ascended in flame and smoke during that wild moment of heart-revealing candor.

"There's nothing I can say, of course," began the man, brokenly. "I did not mean to be a traitor to Preston. But at such a time—" he paused and laid his hand on hers. "Florence, you felt it, too—you understand!"

She nodded her head silently. She would not meet his eyes. She had turned and was persistently gazing out of the window at the shifting lights and shadows of the street.

"When I saw you there, alone, with the smoke swirling about you, and with that dear light in your eyes—there was nothing in all the world but just you. All these past long months were as if they had not been. I forgot Preston, his love for you, and the reason why I had left you."

She stirred suddenly. "And is that—why—you came away?" she asked.

"Yes, I was trying to play square. I found out how Preston felt, and I knew then that I must not stay."

She laughed a little shyly. "But you didn't seem to take me into consideration," she murmured.

He sighed and shook his head. "I didn't think I needed to. I didn't see how any girl could help caring for Preston—when he cared so much for her."

"But I never cared for him that way," she protested. "Besides, I've been doing my best to make him care for someone else."

A quick joy shone in the man's eyes. "And have you?—will he?—can she—?" As he stopped, helplessly, the girl laughed.

"That's exactly the trouble! 'Have I?'—'will he?'—and 'can she?' They are questions I ask myself a dozen times a day. It is Madge Dana, you know, and she's a dear. I think he's beginning to think so, himself, too—a little. I hope so. Anyway, I told him two months ago that I knew now I could never care for him—that way."

The man leaned forward eagerly.

"You've told him that—already?"

"Yes."

"Then I—Florence!" He was trying to look into her face, but she still kept it steadily from him. "Florence, then your eyes did tell me the truth back in the corridor, and I may be—as rapturously contented as I please?" he finished softly.

She hesitated, then drew in her breath with a little tremulous break, as she turned and looked straight into his eyes and gave a little nod, and the next moment she was sobbing in his arms.